WHAT REMAINS

COREY NILES

Crystal Lake Publishing
Where Stories Come Alive!

www.crystallakepub.com

WELCOME
TO ANOTHER

CRYSTAL LAKE PUBLISHING
CREATION

Join today at www.crystallakepub.com & www.patreon.com/CLP

*For Pop-Pop, Raymond Joseph "Joe" Lewis, 1944 – 2023.
Thank you for teaching me to enjoy the ride,
especially when it's against the wind.*

PART ONE

BEFORE

I

The farm is lost in the juxtaposition of desperate abandonment and stubborn existence that infects so much of the world on the verge of the White. Within another day, the yellow farmhouse, red barn, overgrown yard, and rotting silo will be consumed by the billowing wall of clouds from which no one and nothing has ever returned.

Sebastian and I will be gone by then. We're going to survive.

I hit the brakes, and the Kawasaki Vulcan bounces to a stop on the gravel road in front of the house. Sebastian grips me a little tighter. I hate how much it reminds me of before, of when more than an uneven road brought his body close to mine. I stop the train of thought there. What happened before the White isn't important now. We'll deal with it on the other side of this mess.

I put my feet down, and he steps off the bike. He hands me the rifle without a second glance. Tucking his overgrown hair behind his ears, he brings the binoculars up to his eyes to get a better look at the farm. It casts even more of a shadow on his sunken cheeks. The road and the sporadic food along the way have hardened his boyish features.

I strap the rifle over my shoulder and walk the bike to the cornfield across the road to stash it among the dried husks. The place looks abandoned, but the owners or a passerby could still be waiting to shoot us to kingdom come. Or steal what little food and gasoline we have secured to the bike. Or worse.

Back on the road, I take the rifle in my hands and squeeze the barrel to stop it from shaking. Like Sebastian and my views on gun control, my anti-anxiety medication didn't last long in the face of the White and all the insanity that erupted in its wake. No one cares about refilling prescriptions when the world is ending.

"You okay?" Sebastian asks in a perfunctory manner that we both know is out of obligation. It stings worse than silence.

"I'm fine," I say, a little too sharp. In an attempt to smooth things over, I add, "This place looks like it could be on the cover of some rustic home journal, you know? One all water stained in a doctor's office."

"Yeah." He sounds tired. He lowers the binoculars from his face and lets them hang from the band around his neck. Then, he removes the machete from the sheath that's secured to his belt. We found it back in Pennsylvania, and he thankfully hasn't had a reason to use it yet. "Well, I don't see any obvious red flags. Looks empty."

"We should get to it then." I take a deep breath, reminding myself that we've made it this far and that we will continue to make it. We're just going to get some supplies and move on—no different than the dozen places before it. Plus, these back roads are safer. That's why we're taking them. Even if someone's here, they'll probably just tell us to leave before they'd waste the bullets on two scrawny twenty-some-thing men, right?

I try to ignore the urge to vomit. The sewing pin in my pocket calls to me. A single jab in my thigh, and the pain would pull me out of the *Choose Your Own Demise* adventure book that is drafting itself in my mind. But there is no way I can get to the pin now without lowering the gun and alerting Sebastian.

I steel myself and head up the sidewalk. Sebastian surveys everything behind us. I focus on the house. The sheer curtains on the first and second floors reveal no lookouts. I check the stairs and front porch for tripwires, hoping to spot them in the afternoon light before we're ensnared or blown to bits. Nothing. A windowpane in the front door, however, is broken. Other vultures made it to this body before us. If we're lucky, they're long gone and didn't pick the bones clean.

I try the doorknob. Unlocked. I push it open, surprised that it doesn't expel an eerie creak. Not that the house needs it. Shrouded in darkness beyond a rectangle of light from the front door, the place is creepy enough in its own right.

I step inside to the left and will my eyes to adjust to the darkness. Something glints across the room. I point the rifle at it before recognizing it for what it is—the glass of a picture frame on a wall reflecting the sunlight. It's of a middle-aged couple with a husky, teenage boy and a small girl with knee-length hair who can't be older than six or seven.

I push thoughts of what became of the family away. A quaint living room comes into view. A couch, covered in plastic, sits between two intricately carved wooden end tables. No one appears to be crouching around the furniture to ambush us. Across the room behind me, a wooden entertainment stand holds more pictures of the family, knick-knacks, and a clunky square TV.

I turn back to Sebastian, who stands in the doorway. He holds the machete out in front of him like a lightsaber. He starts toward the dark hallway to the right where the rest of the house is waiting for us.

I spot a light switch on the wall at the start of the hallway. I can't help trying it. I flip the switch back and forth. *Click, click. Click, click.* We both have flashlights, but I was hoping—despite reason—that farther south, with a little more distance between us and the White, some semblance of old delicacies like power might remain.

I don't realize I'm still flipping the switch until Sebastian lays a hand on mine and shushes me. I fight the impulse to spout some cutting remark about being sorry for hoping for some luck. He's right. We need to listen for anyone else in the house. He takes out his flashlight and points it down the hall, revealing a faded yellow fridge in what must be the kitchen. I begrudgingly take out my flashlight and, holding it close to the barrel, follow behind him.

A shut door to our left leads to a coat closet. The door to our right is a beach-themed bathroom with shell-covered decorations and a starfish soap dispenser. Once making sure both are empty, we head to the kitchen. We need to collect what we can before exploring the rest of the place in case we have to make a speedy exit.

The window above a porcelain sink, which is covered in a sheer curtain, faintly illuminates the small room. Glass and ceramic shards crunch under our feet. The cabinets are all thrown open and whatever wasn't food in them now apparently covers the floor. Whoever showed up before us wasn't happy with their bounty.

Another doorway beside the fridge leads to the back of the house. I keep it in the corner of my eye while I open the fridge. I'm greeted with a waft of rot. Molding meat and cheese. Liquefied fruit. Rotting vegetables. My mouth thickens with saliva as stomach acid crawls up my throat. I slam the door shut and swallow hard to push it back down. The burning sensation makes me cough.

"Power must have been out for a while." I step back to distance myself from the smell and almost trip on a shattered half of a plate.

"I think it's safe to say we probably won't find any places with power going forward." He's on the tops of his toes, reaching blindly into one of the high cabinets across the room with his free hand. It comes back empty.

I don't remind him that last week, I found a few apples that were salvageable in a fridge that someone was using for storage. We spent the better half of yesterday bickering, and the thought of repeating it today, while also probably finding no food, seems exhausting.

I join him in checking the cabinets. The previous scavengers were thorough. All I find is flaking cabinet liner. Sebastian does snag a dry packet wedged in the back of an empty Lazy Susan. He inspects it with his flashlight. "World's best family-style turkey gravy."

"Yum," I say dryly.

"Fuck." He tosses it aside in frustration, but when we leave the kitchen, he goes back for it before I have the chance. If we keep getting this lucky, we're going to need it.

We continue through the house, each room in this unknown maze presenting a new potential end of our travels. One after another, we find them unoccupied, but it only makes me fear that we are homing in on where the squatters are waiting to ensnare us.

The dirt floor basement just has an empty wire stand for canned goods. The master bedroom and bathroom in the back of the house were already ravaged. Wooden dresser drawers capsized in a sea of discarded clothes. I find some gauze in the bathroom that I stuff into my pocket, but that's it.

Upstairs, there are two bedrooms and a second bath. Sebastian digs out a Swiss Army knife from behind a bean bag in the boy's room, which has also been upturned in a previous, frantic search. The little girl's room is strangely preserved. Pepto Bismol pink walls, white wicker furniture, stacks of picture books, and clusters of stuffed animals—all placed with the intention of an IKEA-staged room.

The sight of it stops Sebastian in his tracks. "You don't think she—"

"I bet whoever came through before us figured they weren't going to find anything of worth in here." I turn to leave, but he remains in the doorway. "Come on."

"You're probably right." He tears himself away from the room and shuts the door behind us.

We return downstairs, and Sebastian goes back to the master bedroom.

I follow him. "What are you looking for?"

"It's time to retire my shirt. It stinks. Going to find a new one since there doesn't seem to be anything else worth taking in this shithole." He picks through the clothes on the floor before going to the closet.

I almost mention the gauze, but it doesn't seem like he wants a silver lining right now. I can hardly blame him. I'd be lying if I didn't admit the disappointment at yet another fruitless detour. I sniff the Harley-Davidson T-shirt I snagged from a gas station yesterday. It still isn't too bad.

The sun is getting low outside. We should get back on the road before too long if we want to get some more miles in before we find somewhere to sleep. "I'll go check out the barn while you do that."

"If you want to give me a minute, I can come with you." He pokes his head out of the closet. His old shirt is already off, and his hairy chest is in clear view.

I stare at him. Even with gaunt features, I don't think I've seen a more beautiful man. All I can think about is how for nearly five years, I was fortunate enough to lay my head on that chest each night. Then, I look at the floor. Because that was before I ruined it. Before the White showed up. Before everything went to hell.

My eyes well up with regret. I start out of the room. "If anyone's here, I think we would've found them by now."

I dry my eyes. Now isn't the time for this. If I'm ever going to get the chance of fixing what I broke with Sebastian, I'll have to make sure we survive the White and keep ahead of it. I go out the back door and across a field of tall grass to the barn.

It looks like it is one strong wind away from collapsing. The pale red paint on the old wood slats has peeled back like bloody hangnails. The barn doors are shut. The chances of a firing squad waiting for me to open the doors so they can riddle me with bullets are slim, but the thought still crosses my mind. I lift the latch and let them fling open.

Flies swarm me. Legs scurry across my face and fluttering wings buzz in my ears. Batting them away, I spot people overhead. They're jumping down from the loft. I stumble back, screaming. I point the rifle in their direction and squeeze the trigger.

It resists.

I forgot to take off the damn safety.

I scramble to remove it, but they aren't dropping to the ground. They're floating in the air. I point the flashlight at them. The light dances in my unsteady hand. Three people hang from nooses secured to the rafters. While the older man and woman look like the ones in the family portrait, the boy is much taller and thinner. He must've hit a growth spurt before they—

I shut my eyes, but I already saw too much of their purple, bloated faces to erase the sight of them. And the boy. It looked like something gnawed on his face. There was a chunk of flesh missing from his cheek and the white of his teeth within glinted in the flashlight.

Oh god, they must've all gone over the edge together. The White took thousands long before it reached them, and it devoured these four as well. Only, I don't think I saw the girl. Against my better judgment, I shine my light back up at them. There's a rope tied to a rafter beside the man, but the end of it is frayed. I check the hay-covered ground below for her body. Nothing's there.

The girl's pristine room returns to me, and my stomach turns. The rope could've broken when they all jumped. She could've watched her whole family die. I wonder if she was still here when whoever broke into the house before us destroyed the place. If so, she might still be here now, hiding from us and slowly starving to death.

No.

We are losing daylight.

That's what I should worry about.

I pull the collar of my shirt over my nose to diminish the smell of decay. I keep my head down and search through the barn, wiping away the sweat on my forehead that the flies seem determined to stick to as I go. There are a few farm tools along the one wall and a rusting tractor toward the back that doesn't look like it's run in a decade. I still open the gas cap and smell for ethanol. Only death pervades the air.

I should've just shut the doors as soon as I opened them, but I wanted to find something other than gravy and gauze. I don't look up at the family on my way out. I focus on the yellow fields in the distance. A cold autumn breeze rushes to meet me, and the wood groans overhead as the bodies sway. Outside, I take what feels like my first breath in minutes before I latch the doors.

There, back pressed against the barn, I drop the rifle and rub my eyes, foolishly hoping I can scrub that image from my thoughts. My breaths shorten, and I know if I don't start breathing normally soon, a panic attack is imminent. I don't want to think about the family or the panic attack or anything.

I reach into my pocket, grab the pin by its round plastic top, and jam it as hard as I can into my thigh. Everything evaporates in the sharp, sudden pain that radiates from the spot. I savor the relief as I pull the pin back out and, after dropping it into my pocket, rub the wound with my pointer finger for the aftershocks. Later, when Sebastian falls asleep, I will dab it with rubbing alcohol to sterilize it and get another extra sting before bed.

The shame follows the relief. I tell myself the constellation of red dots on my thighs is better than the ragged knife scars that covered them after high school. This is better than drinking or taking random drugs that will prevent me from remaining alert. Once I find my medication at another pharmacy, I'm going to stop.

Minutes pass before I stand. I'm relieved to find that if the blood stained my black jeans, it isn't noticeable.

Sebastian doesn't need to see what's in the barn. It'll crush him, and he will undoubtedly want to look for the girl. Try to help her. Give her a portion of our dwindling food supply. His compassion for others was something I always admired, but it's too short-sighted for this new world. Whatever fate befell her, it's probably best not to know. And we don't have enough resources or room on the bike for anyone else.

I walk back to the house. The White looms overhead behind me. Even being a day away, the undulating clouds emit enough light to cast my shadow down on the grass in front of me. Every second we spend on this barren farm, it's inching closer to us. It's time for us to get back on the road.

I expect Sebastian to be waiting outside, dressed in some oversized T-shirt. He's nowhere in sight. I pick up the pace a little. The nagging thought that I know better than to split up races in my mind, juxtaposed with the family, nooses taut around their necks and hands joined, dropping from the hay loft to their deaths.

I hurry into the master bedroom. There's only a pile of discarded clothes in the closet. I rush out of the room.

"Sebastian!" Panic coats my words.

"Up here," he calls from above me. His voice sounds normal, but I take the steps two at a time. He's in the hall with something in his hand over his head.

"You scared," I say, catching my breath, "the shit out of me."

"You're the one who wanted to check the barn. Look what I found. Something came through a second ago. I'm trying to get a better signal."

He holds a small, silver, AM/FM radio in his hand that hisses white noise.

"Where did you find that?"

"In the back of the closet with some random things. There were batteries in the entertainment stand. Find anything in the barn?"

"Nothing but hay and an old tractor," I say as nonchalantly as I can.

"Great. Wait. Listen." He moves his arm to the left and a woman's voice comes through, staticky and distorted, but comprehendible. It's a recording. We listen to it the whole way through several times, speechless.

My name is Tiffany Rodrigues. I am a geologist who is living in Miami. I am recording this broadcast on July eighteenth, 2027. I will play it on a loop for as long as I can, and I pray that those who hear it can share this message.

Wherever you are, please know that not all hope is lost. The White may be increasing in acceleration since it originated at the Poles, but its destination is the same as ever. The two halves shall meet at the equator, and if there is a sanctuary or a solution to be found, we will bear witness to it there.

We are preparing flights to Ecuador, and we will continue searching for more survivors to take on this voyage until the White nears. You can find us at the WLRN Public Radio and Television Building each morning at dawn, where we will be vetting potential passengers.

We hope to see you there.

Eventually, the recording stops. There must not have been much juice left in the batteries. Sebastian tosses the radio aside. The air in the hallway is heavy. Like the radio waves were somehow tangible and filled the room from the shaggy blue carpet to the popcorn ceiling. My heart pounds in my chest at a rate that is somehow faster than the thoughts racing in my mind. A geologist. A plane. A possible way of surviving this mess. The first glimpse of hope in the despair that's overwhelmed us since the White started spreading.

Whatever Sebastian sees in my face, he doesn't like it. He sighs. "It was recorded almost two months ago. She sounded like she's one of those looney-tune cult members. What'd you call them again?"

"White Standers." I don't think she sounds insane though. "She sounded sincere to me. And she said—"

"She said they're vetting passengers. Probably looking for more useful people than us. Plus, every person who's heard this is probably rushing there. I'd be shocked if they haven't torn apart those planes already. If there even are planes."

His words drip with such uncharacteristic, heated cynicism that I don't even know how to respond. It's more than he's said all day, and he's the one who wants to help every poor asshole we come across. Not just after the White. Ever since we became best friends in third grade, he's always had a stray or two trailing behind him. The kid with bifocal goggles in middle school. The older widow in our apartment building who liked playing poker. More recently, the hungry boy we came across near the West Virginia/Pennsylvania state border. The list is endless.

I come close to asking him why a voice on a radio is any different than someone we pass along the road, wanting to see what's preventing

Sebastian from hoping that our lives could be more than this scavenging. But I don't. I'm afraid I already know the answer. I'm the one who taught him that the other shoe could always drop. "You, ah, think so?"

"Probably some cruel woman at a nearby radio station, getting everyone vying for local resources away from her."

I know he could be right. I also know we've been fleeing the White for so long, all the while racing toward the other half of it. We haven't been doing anything except biding our time. Running away from the inevitable and praying the White will vanish as suddenly as it appeared before we starve or are killed.

"We're heading south now. The only difference is that rather than running away, we will be running toward something. We've been hoping for a miracle. Maybe this is it. Where are the maps?" I start down the stairs.

Sebastian follows me. "We're barely keeping a day ahead of the White now. Miami is a far way from bumfuck nowhere West Virginia when we have to stop two or three times a day to find gas and food. If they haven't already packed those planes, which might not even be real, I doubt they're going to have free spots if we get there."

"We can't find fuel and food because we've been avoiding highways and cities," I say, not looking behind me as I pass through the first floor and go out onto the front porch.

"Because this way's safer. That was your idea, in case you forgot. Do you really want a repeat of New York?"

I shrug off the awful memory and the fact that I'm usually the more cautious one in my excitement. This is worth the risk. "We can still avoid *major* cities. Even just using the highway more would cut down on our time. Before, we could've made the trip in a long day or two."

"*Before* being the key word."

I strap the rifle on my back and pull the motorcycle out of the corn. I didn't realize how tightly I was gripping the gun until I have to force my cramped fingers to work so that I can search the compartments and bags secured to the bike for the maps. Sebastian is in charge of them. After looking for a minute without luck, I turn back to him.

Arms crossed, he says, "Side pocket to the left. No. Your other left."

I open it on the leather seat. Trace the path all the way down to Miami. "We could take I-77 and I-95. Make some stops at slightly larger towns for gas. Probably find some real food too. We could make it there in a few days easy."

"We'll be putting ourselves in more danger for at what best could be described as a long shot. I mean, this whole thing could be a trap." There are tears in his eyes. I haven't seen an emotion besides contempt or exhaustion on his face for so long that it takes me aback.

"It's a chance." My words shake in a sudden rush of emotion that I don't fully understand beyond feeling like I'm close to tears. "I know this may be a lie or a trap or a million things, but what alternative do we have?"

"We could try to enjoy ourselves. The next time we find a good stash of food and maybe some booze, we could drive a little farther that day and take the next to relax a little bit." He turns back to the house.

I'd give anything for a day like that. A day when every single breath and thought isn't consumed with keeping us alive. But if we are just going to lie around and pretend the White isn't going to kill us, then we might as well go join the family in the barn.

No. We have to keep going.

I want to wrap my arms around him, but I'm not sure how he'll react. "We will have the rest of our lives to enjoy ourselves if this works out. We can't give up now. I promise I won't let anything bad happen to you."

There's a long pause. "Don't make promises you can't keep, Alex."

I flinch at the words.

He looks back, cheeks growing red. "I mean with the whole bad things happening to us. You can't control that."

"Yeah. I know," I say, somehow feeling worse about it now than when I thought it was a jab. He turns to the house. I wonder if there will ever be a time when there isn't this tension. When we will return to the way we were before that night in the living room. "How about this? I promise to do everything in my power to keep us safe, babe."

My old pet name for him leaves my mouth automatically, before I can stop it.

He freezes.

I should cut my tongue out. Trying to push past it, I add, "We can have that wonderful day in Ecuador. Food and booze. The whole works. Okay?"

He turns back, an eyebrow raised. "What does the *whole works* include?"

"You're just going to have to wait to find out." I wink at him. "Okay?"

His eyebrow remains arched, but I can see his resolve waning. "I still think it's a bad idea. But . . ."

"Okay?" I can't hide the excitement in my voice.

"Okay."

I replay the geologist's words, and I almost believe them.

All hope is not lost.

<u>PART TWO</u>

WHITE STANDERS

I

Morning light stains the gas station bathroom in a sepia tone. I crane my neck to look at the door. Sebastian was supposed to wake me up before dawn so we could get on the road. But he isn't sitting next to the door. In fact, the rifle leans against the wall alone—like he dissolved into the tiled wall while I slept.

I push myself up to peer around the room. Seatless toilet in the corner. Baby changing table hanging on for dear life on the wall. Ravaged condom dispenser beside the door. Bike in front of the toilet. And Sebastian?

Something shifts its weight in front of me. Someone. Sebastian is curled up in the crescent moon that my body forms lying on my side. His soft snore comes out as more of a purr. I feel him shivering outside of the sleeping bag. This autumn is a lot colder than the last. I swallow the anger that burns at the thought that if someone kicked in the door, we would've been defenseless. Instead, I pull him closer. He stirs for a moment, whispering something, and dozes off.

We fell asleep adjacent to one another in shifts for months. This is the first time his body has been pressed to mine in a while. It's bizarre how used to sleeping beside another person I became that, when I moved to the couch, I clutched decorative pillows for something to hold on to at night.

We haven't slept like this since the first research team entered the White in Antarctica. Some renegade journalist released the live body-camera footage of one of the researchers. Blinding light and screams of those who were moving into it. Not of shock or fear. Of pain—like the damn thing was eating them alive.

Back then, we thought we had years—hell, decades—before the White would reach us. A pestering reminder of doom that, highlighted in the cries of some of the brightest minds of the generation, compelled Sebastian to lead me back to our bed that night. We slept together. Afterward, I spooned him, and he pulled my arms around him. A normalcy we both took comfort in that night.

The next evening, after he headed to bed, I tried the doorknob, but the door was locked. We never discussed it. I returned to sleeping on the couch and understood this wasn't the first step in rebuilding what I broke. It was an exception to our estrangement. An emotional lapse in judgment.

Those early days before the riots are like a dream now. Another strange existence that was separate from the world we knew and the horrors we couldn't have imagined would come to pass. So, I hold him now. I hold on to that momentary reprieve that made him forget how I ruined us. And, comforted with the hope of the radio message, the SPAM in my stomach that we found in the gas station under a line of shelves, and the knowledge that we siphoned enough gas to drive for a few hours once we get up soon, I drift back to sleep.

II

Knocking. That's what pulls me from the disjointed vignettes of my stress dreams. Then, the warmth and weight of Sebastian vanishes, and he shakes my shoulder. I open my eyes. Sebastian's panicked face is even more ashen in the muted afternoon light. The sight of him sobers me from the grogginess of sleep.

Knock, knock, knock.

Reality sets in.

We've slept through the day. Most of the fucking day.

Knock, knock, knock.

Oh god.

The White. It'll be nearing us. We've only been able to keep a day ahead of it at our current pace. And there's someone at the door.

Knock, knock, knock.

The weight of it all tightens the hold of panic around my throat. I cough in a poor attempt to mask the gagging and swallow whatever's trying to exit my system. I can't freak out. I need to act.

The knocking starts again, permeating the little bathroom. I don't know how I could be stupid enough to fall back asleep this morning. Especially when we stayed in a gas station a stone's throw from the highway—far closer to civilization than we've dared to go in a long time. A gamble I hoped would pay off when we reached Miami in a day or two.

I'm so mad that I don't know what to do. We've worked our asses off just to distance ourselves from the White, and to think it had all been wasted on a couple more hours of sleep makes me want to scream. Makes me want to rip open the door and break the fingers of whoever keeps fucking knocking.

Sebastian loops the machete sheath onto his belt. In a low voice, he says, "I was cold. I fell asleep and—"

"Stop," I whisper, hoping whoever is knocking will lose interest and go away.

"I can hear you." The man's voice is soft and gentle in a strained manner that raises the question of why he's trying so hard to appear harmless.

This is bad.

Fuck, fuck, fuck, I think in beat to the knocks. I hope the man is alone but know that is unlikely. Lone wolves don't make it long in this world. I want to close my eyes, jab my thigh with the pin, and think, but there is no time for that now.

I scramble to my feet. Roll up my sleeping bag. Hand it to Sebastian, who secures it to the motorcycle. Grab the gun. Make sure the safety is off. Squeezing the rifle for dear life, and ordering myself not to vomit, I yell, "Fuck off!"

No immediate response.

Sebastian has his machete in one hand and the handle of the bike in the other. We stand there, waiting for a response.

After what feels like an eternity, the man says, "We mean you no harm."

We.

Sebastian's eyes widen, coming to the same realization.

We could mean one or two other people. It could also mean a group. Enough to overpower us, even with a rifle and a machete. Enough to kill us. Take what little food and supplies we have left and—I stop myself there. No. This isn't where our journey ends. I pat the pocket of my coat where I've saved a dozen extra bullets. The rest are in a compartment on the bike.

I'm digging out the bullets when Sebastian says, "We don't want any trouble. We will be on our way, and no one will get hurt."

His voice is firm. More masculine than usual. A tone I've only heard him use when speaking to his father before he and the rest of our families cut us off. Stuffing my pockets with bullets, I add, "We're armed."

"We are not," the man says. "We mean you no harm."

The repetition of the phrase hardly fills me with confidence of its sincerity. There's something about his speech pattern—a forced reassurance and presentation—that brings me back to Sunday mornings in Connecticut. The smell of wood polish from the pews. Traded glances between Sebastian and me. The pastor prattling on about whatever sin we were inevitably committing that week.

None of which will help us in our current predicament.

I refocus. "I'm going to open the door," I whisper to Sebastian. "You're going to wheel the bike out, and I'm going to cover us. Then, we're going to drive the hell out of here."

Sebastian nods. His clenched jaw makes the muscles in his neck more defined.

I rip open the door. A white face floats in the doorway in front of us. I jump back and somehow will my finger not to pull the trigger. Sebastian gasps. The thick paint on the man's face cracks as he smirks. "The White is nearing. We will be forming a line soon. Our chain will be stronger with another pair of links."

White Standers. A name I dubbed them when they first showed up on the news after the White took Canada. Unlike the living dead White Walkers in *Game of Thrones*, they are more of an infuriating nuisance and a testament to the idiocy of man than a real threat. They don't even walk. They just collect as many unlucky assholes as they can and stand in a line like pale and suicidal Hands Across America participants as the White swallows them. They claim to be peaceful, focusing on free will and accepting God's plan, but they were heavy-handed in New York.

I should've known they'd be swarming this close to the White. No different than the flies in that barn. The man wears what must be a light bed sheet that he's fashioned into a robe. He's closer than Sebastian and I have been to another person in ages. His eyes are what bother me though. Lifeless. Eyes that have seen oblivion and want nothing more than to be part of it.

"Move." I force air in and out of my nostrils to try to fight away the lightheaded feeling that's taking over and making this whole thing seem like a bad dream.

"The White is God's reckoning. Only truly despicable sinners would be afraid of stepping into it and letting the light decide their fate." The sick bastard's smile widens to show yellowed, overlapping front teeth. "If you are good people, then why would you fear it?"

I raise the rifle and point it at his chest. The gun shakes in my unsteady hands.

"Alexander," Sebastian pleads, but I don't waver. I'd sooner blast this fucker into next week than risk him keeping us here.

The man backs away, and I sweep the room. *Breathe in.* Another White Stander is behind the counter, rustling through something out of sight. *Breathe out.* The path to the door is clear. I step aside so Sebastian can get the bike through the bathroom door, and I follow behind him.

Outside, I can feel the White nearing. There is a force to it. A gravitational pull. Wind rushes north, pulling bits of trash and dried leaves through the air and making it hard to capture oxygen in my starved lungs.

There's another aspect to it as well. A longing that takes root. A question of if accepting it would enable it to show mercy upon us. I can't tell if our minds are unable to comprehend such a damning force of nature or if it is somehow sentient, drawing us in.

For a moment, I'm back in the garage with Philip. I can't be older than twelve or thirteen. He wipes sweat from his forehead, leaving a streak of grease across his face. He's gained a little weight since his release, and it makes me happy that I can no longer see the contours of his skull. He's smiling as he tells me again and again that the wrenches I present to him are the wrong size for the bolt he's trying to tighten on his bike.

I stuff the memory away. It's surely a trick of the White.

It's descending to our left. Almost too bright to look at directly. The clouds move about like cream in a cup of coffee. Twisting and turning as they eat the world around them. The parking lot of abandoned cars ahead is lit in a fluorescent light that would be more appropriate in a hospital. We aren't going to be able to drive off in earnest until we reach the road, and the space between us and it is littered in White Standers among the cars and other bits of abandoned trash.

We're exposed in every sense of the word. I hold on desperately to my rifle like it's a life raft in an ocean storm to prevent myself from drowning in the real possibility that we could die before we make it out of here.

Sebastian must come to the same conclusion because he starts for an opening between a car and a gas pump. I look back as I follow. *In.* The white face from the bathroom now looms in the doorway of the gas station. His smile hasn't wavered. *Out.* On either side of us, more are nearing. A short woman with a baby in her arms to our left. Another man to our right. All advancing toward us at a dizzying speed. We aren't anywhere near the road.

The nausea returns, and I can't hide the gagging. Sebastian turns to me, and I bark, "We gotta hurry."

"I'm trying," he says, breathless.

We're almost to the opening. I steal another glance behind us. The two from inside the gas station are approaching, and the others on either side of us are closing ranks.

The woman bounces the baby, who is wrapped in a white blanket, as she walks. They're going to be dead before nightfall.

She catches my gaze. "I think it'll be as painless as falling asleep."

I walk right into a wall and almost lose my footing. I grip it with my free hand for balance. Not a wall. Sebastian. He's stopped dead in his tracks. A bulbous man, whose white hair matches the powder on his face, has his arms stretched out, blocking our way out of here.

"Now, sons." He pauses to look back and forth at us, wasting even more of our limited time.

"Please. We are trying to get through," Sebastian says.

He doesn't move. "Let's talk this over. I have a few boys your age myself."

I don't know if I have enough air in my lungs to speak, but I try. I move the barrel of the gun to his forehead. "Step. The fuck. Aside. Or you'll never get a chance to see your precious White."

He stands his ground.

"Step aside!" I scream. I can hear footsteps behind us. The others must be only a yard away.

"Now you're old enough to know better than to shoot a firearm at a gas station. You're lucky I'm here to—"

A scream. Pounding footsteps. I swing around to see where they are coming from and turn back just in time to watch someone tackle the man to the ground.

Whatever is happening is secondary to the fact that our way is now unblocked.

I elbow Sebastian. "Go!"

We run. The large man screams as a smaller man, dressed in a hoodie and jeans, lands a few punches on him. Whatever is going on between them is none of our business. Ahead, there are one or two White Standers, but they're nowhere close. The path to the road is relatively clear.

Sebastian is so focused on the scene behind us that he trips on a divot in the blacktop and staggers.

"Come on. We're almost out." I inspect the ground ahead before stealing a glance behind us. The smiling White Standers from inside pulls the man off, and the man headbutts the fucker to free himself.

Sebastian slows to a stop. His hair jerks across his forehead in the wind. "He helped us. We should return the favor."

I try to hide how close I am to screaming. "We don't know why he did that. Maybe he's one of his sons. Who cares? He seems like he can handle himself. Come on."

Sebastian rolls his eyes, like the White isn't descending. Like these White Standers couldn't take our bike. Like death isn't breathing down our necks. He stays where he is and doesn't say a word. I peer around. I can navigate the rest of the obstructions on the bike. I throw the gun over my shoulder and take the bike from him. "Get on. Let's go."

I sit and start up the bike. Over the engine, I can hear someone screaming. I look back. While the White Standers are still huddled near the pumps, licking their wounds, the man is rushing toward us. "Wait! Please, God, wait!"

Shit.

I look away from him. Bury the idea of helping him. It's too dangerous. The White is too close. I turn my attention to Sebastian. "Get on the bike. Please. It'll be here soon."

Sebastian remains still. I cut the engine, remove the key, then put on the kickstand. I take the gun back as the man nears. He slows, raising his hands. He can't be more than a few years older than us. He's heaving air, and his words come out in sporadic bursts between breaths. "Please. It's my boy. He's back. At my house. You have to. Take him with you. Those psychos trashed our car. He'll die here. I can't let him. Die here."

Sebastian's back is to me. Who knows what he's thinking, but I say something before he has the chance. "We appreciate the help, but we don't have the room or the supplies. We are leaving. Sebastian, come on."

"He's three. Please. He'll fit. My house is just over there." He points toward a line of houses on the other side of the street that are blanched in the descending light. His focus is on Sebastian, who must look more sympathetic, but he's getting close to us and the bike.

My cheeks are going numb from the lack of oxygen. *In.* I aim the gun at him. *Out.* "Back off."

His nostrils flare. He isn't scared. He's pissed. "Please. He's just a kid."

The group of White Standers starts toward us, two with splashes of red staining their robes. The man broke their calm demeanor. More and more by the second, I feel like we are one false move from losing everything. That's all I can think about when I say to Sebastian, "You already slept through your shift. You'll get us killed. Get on the bike. If this guy even has a son, I'm sure there are more people waiting at his house to take the bike and our belongings and leave us to die."

Sebastian faces me, blinking, like he just woke up from a trance. Pain wrinkles his face. I'd feel worse about blaming him for our late start if we weren't still in mortal danger.

"Calm down, friend." The man is just a foot away from me.

In. I keep the gun trained on him. *Out.* "I told you to back off."

He puts his hand on the barrel and pushes it down. "If you didn't shoot Father Christmas, I have a feeling I'm in the clear. Probably blanks. And coming with me is the least you can fucking do after I saved y'all."

The anger flares again, and at that moment, he tugs at the gun. Sebastian says something, but all I can think about is how this isn't how we are going to die.

I pull the trigger.

Bang.

The recoil punches me in the shoulder. The weight of the man pulling on the gun disappears. He stares up at me in shock from the ground. There's a pool of blood leaking from his thigh. The only sound is the roaring wind. He dips his hand in the blood. Maroon so dark it almost looks brown, glistening in the light. When he speaks, his words start as a whisper and grow to a howl. "You shot me. You signed my fucking death warrant. You fucking shot me!"

He lurches forward in my direction, but the pain stops him. He grabs his leg and continues to bombard me with insults.

I shot him.

It doesn't make sense in my head.

I never did more than threaten someone with the rifle, and now, I shot a man.

The White Standers are getting close to us. The shot quickened their pace.

I don't feel like I'm here. I'm a specter, floating above the scene. An observer. An anthropologist taking notes. I can't make sense of the man's words anymore. I hand the gun to Sebastian, who is staring at him. He grasps it thoughtlessly.

I can't bring myself to look him in the eyes.

I take a seat and start the engine. "Get on the bike."

His hands wrap around me, but it's different now. He's doing it because it's his only option. A memory resurfaces. I'm standing in the living room of our apartment. I'm crying as I recite the words I carefully planned for days. Sebastian's face slowly turns to stone. Cold marble carved into a look of contempt that a sculptor took months to perfect.

I shake my head to loosen its hold on me. Another game of the White. All these awful memories of before haven't returned since we neared it in New York. A past that won't matter if we can't secure our future. I remind myself that I can still breathe. I take off, and while the bottom of the bike scrapes against the lip of the sidewalk on our way out, we leave this nightmare in the side mirrors.

I don't look back until we soar onto the highway. By the time I do, all that is left to see is the White. The all-consuming nature of it, as far up into the sky as we can see, bears down on us. Somewhere near the gas station, a chain of psychotic paper dolls will greet the unknown with smiles on their faces.

I don't think of the man or the tears that streak my face, traveling horizontally in the wind. I speed up. I don't plan on stopping anytime soon.

III

After we are well into Virginia, I'm able to take control of my breathing again. "If he cared about his son, if he even had one, he would've killed us without hesitating to save him."

Sebastian doesn't answer. I think he must be asleep until he says, "You don't know that."

The tears return, blurring the road ahead. I shot him. It wasn't a deadly shot in itself, but leaving him with the White Standers, after what he did to them, with the White nearing, was exactly what he said. I signed his death warrant.

Wind fills my ears after that, and I have to keep telling myself it's from the speed at which we are driving to calm my nerves. We're safe from the White.

Closer to sundown, Sebastian says, "I didn't mean to fall asleep. I don't want to die, but I also want to be able to live with myself if we somehow survive this."

I should tell him the truth. That I was the one who truly doomed us today. That I got too caught up in the past to focus on the road ahead. That I was scared, and I would've told him any lie to get him on the bike.

But the way he lingered in the face of the White makes me reconsider. While I'm sure he wanted to help the man, even if there wasn't anything we could have done that wouldn't have damned us both, there seemed to be more to it. Did the draw of the White somehow make it farther into his system than mine?

If a few fibs are how I'm going to keep him safe, then I'll take them. I was the one who suggested driving closer to civilization, which means it's my responsibility to get us to our destination intact. I have to remain focused on our end goal and leave the past behind us.

It's just until Miami. Once we're safe, I'll tell him the truth about today and apologize on the flight to Ecuador. He'll understand—I'm sure of it—as long as we make it to the planes.

I did what needed to be done. Nothing more. Nothing less. I let the rest go, dropping it on the blacktop and continuing to weave through the abandoned cars on the highway, heading south.

PART THREE

THE END
OF THE
WORLD

I

Sebastian eyes the empty Diet Coke can I placed on a cinder block in the alleyway. His lips press together in a thin line. "What is this?"

We drove for hours in the dark yesterday and stopped a little after we reached North Carolina. I wanted to go farther, but we already burned through half our gas supply. I wondered, perhaps idiotically, if somehow the pull of the White made the bike work harder in those early miles. More likely, driving faster burned through gas at a higher rate than I'm used to at our regular slow and steady pace.

The next day, we got another three hours under our belts before stopping in the suburbs of Charlotte. While the massive, two-door garage we stand behind didn't have much gasoline in the mower, the adjacent house had a decent bounty of canned goods. Bike packed with two cans of soup and another three of assorted vegetables, we were ready to continue on the road when I spotted the Diet Coke can and had an idea.

Now, standing beside Sebastian, I explain myself. "I know you said you don't want to use the gun if you don't have to, but if something like yesterday happens again and for some reason I'm unable to do so, you should know how to use it."

Sebastian's expression darkens. We haven't exchanged more than a few words since we got on the road. "Maybe we should focus on reasoning with people we come across as opposed to pointing and shooting."

I sigh. He knows why we can't trust a single person we meet along the road as well as I do. He sat beside me on our couch, watching as fights over food shortages escalated to mass shootings and break-ins. He fled our apartment building with me when a group of scavengers set it on fire. He observed firsthand how there are far worse groups than the White Standers. People who take advantage of the chaos of the White to live out their most barbaric and brutal fantasies.

I don't remind him of that. Reason didn't keep him from giving a fourth of our food to that boy on the West Virginia/Pennsylvania state border. Instead, I say, "I didn't want to shoot him. He grabbed the gun. Would you have preferred I let him take it? Gave him all our supplies? Joined hands with the looney tunes and skipped happily into the White?"

"All I'm saying is that desperation doesn't have to always bring out the very worst in people." His gaze doesn't leave the Diet Coke can.

"I'll take your word for it. Here." I try to hand him the gun.

"I'm not shooting it." He steps back. "I don't take any pleasure in this macho, *Mad Max* bullshit. You clearly have more of a calling for it."

The bite in his words reignites my frustration. "And if someone kills me. Or we get separated. And it's between you and them, you're just going to do what exactly? A machete is useless against a bullet."

He doesn't respond.

"I'm not enjoying this any more than you are. I'm just trying to keep us alive, and we are only going to be in more danger ahead as we look for gas off the highway, and I can't do this alone." The words come out more forcefully than I intend. I soften my voice. "And if anything, I would totally be a Furiosa. But I'm not shaving my head. Only Charlize Theron can pull off that haircut."

He turns to me, annoyed. "Don't do that."

I almost ask *what*, but I know what I'm doing. During a former blowout—the subject matter of which I've long since forgotten—he stormed off, and I screamed "That's all folks," in a bad Porky Pig impression to cut the tension. It brought him back into the apartment, but he wasn't laughing. *Don't try to sugar coat this and make me the bad guy because you realize you fucked up and are too proud to apologize.*

That wasn't what I was doing, but sure enough, any attempt at levity on my part that he perceives as poorly timed is just a repeat of that moment.

"Fine. Let's be up front then. Ever since we heard that radio message, it's been like pulling teeth to get you to meet me halfway. I don't understand it."

I've gotten closer to him, but still, he stares forward as he speaks. "We don't have enough gas to make it all the way to Miami. We barely have enough food for a few days. And for what? Another day driving on that fucking bike? I haven't given up. I'm just fucking exhausted from this death march that started way before that stupid radio message."

His words take the wind out of me. A gut punch. I step back. Turn away. Stare down the alleyway and try to focus on the gravel and the garages and the house and anything other than the tears that are trying to spill over my lash line. "What's the alternative? Huh?"

"Christ on a cracker." A woman stands between two garages across the alleyway. I fall back into Sebastian in my rush toward the bike. He steadies me with a firm hand. She's clean, holding a steaming mug, dressed in a pastel-yellow sweater and khaki pants with her gray hair teased out in spikes reminiscent of a porcupine. The sight of someone who seems totally unaffected by the White shocks us both. We stand there, staring at her. "Here I was, missing my husband. Thank you, Sid and Nancy, for helping me appreciate the joys of solitude."

"Huh" is all I manage.

"I know I'm quite the sight to behold, boys, but it's rude to stare. Even ruder to interrupt my morning tea with this nonsense." She keeps an eye on us over the ridge of her mug as she sips it.

"We were just leaving." I start toward the bike, but Sebastian stays put.

"You need gasoline?" the woman asks.

I answer in the negative at the same time Sebastian says, "We do."

The woman assesses us. "You know how to use a hammer?"

"Yeah," he says.

I'm honestly not sure if he's lying or not. "We have to get going."

"I have more gasoline and food than you'll be able to carry on that bike, and I have shelter for the night."

If only to prove to Sebastian she's lying, I ask, "And why would you share it with two strangers you just met?"

"I'm a good Christian woman." She raises a hand. Her fingers are riddled with arthritis, twisted and bent in violent angles like tangled tree roots. "And I can't use a hammer."

"We have to go. The White—"

"Will probably be here sometime tomorrow in the early afternoon if the few radio tracking transmissions I've caught are correct," she says.

"Great. Lead the way!" Sebastian starts across the gravel.

It takes me a second to realize he's serious. "Sebastian!"

"I'm going with—What's your name?"

"Debbie. Follow me. I'd like to be done before dusk. I have quite the night planned." I can't see her face because she's already turned around. Still, it's not hard to imagine a menacing look. *Quite the night planned?* This has trap written all over it in bold red letters.

I want to grab Sebastian and tell him that old women are very much as capable of theft, homicide, and cannibalism as anyone. However, something tells me this has way more to do with proving a point than trusting her. He slips between the two garages behind her.

"Fuck," I say, loud enough to hopefully reach them. I strap the gun over my shoulder and trail them with the bike. I keep my distance but remain close enough to hopefully interject when she and whoever she's probably working with try to kill Sebastian.

All the unique and creative ways we could be slaughtered or imprisoned in these suburbs fill my thoughts. I take a deep breath of crisp air and try to bury the rage. I have to stay alert. The woman crosses a yard, turns right, and leads us down a street lined with uncannily similar houses. Two-story boxes with wrap-around porches and two-door garages. Beige and white with the occasional muted navy or army green. Photocopies in rows on either side of us like some sort of funhouse mirror.

The whole place seems like a graveyard. A monument to the old world. No broken glass or charred structures. The worst I see is knee-length lawns that only make the imported grass look lusher. It's all so different from the destruction I've grown accustomed to that it only heightens the strange nature of this place.

Why the hell was this block spared of the chaos that has torn apart every other place we've come across? Was it deserted early on for beach houses and summer homes? Did the residents flee for the southern border like every wild animal that wasn't chained up or domesticated beyond the point of recognizing their basic survival instincts? Or maybe the residents are hanging from nooses inside their homes. Spacious coffins for families of four.

The woman raises the mug to her mouth and tips the remainder back before considering it and smashing it on the blacktop. Even watching it happen, the sound in the otherwise silent street surprises me. Sebastian flinches. The woman cackles. "Sorry. I have enough mugs to keep me until the White demolishes this street tomorrow, and frankly, I always hated that one."

Sebastian laughs, but I can hear the strain in his voice. I guess the end of the world is affecting her. My eyes bore into the back of his head, hoping I can somehow will reason into his stubborn mind with mere concentrated thought alone. If we aren't murdered, I'm going to kill him for putting our lives in jeopardy out of spite. Helping people along the way and blindly trusting every desperate person we come across are two very different things. Both dangerous. One deadly.

I navigate the bike around the shattered ceramic and continue behind them.

"Here we are," the woman says when she reaches the very last house on the street. It's similar in structure to the others, but the yard shows defection. The trunk of the maple tree in the front yard has a knitted, rainbow sweater around it. Little painted peace signs, dreamcatchers, and windchimes hang from the branches.

She leads Sebastian up the sidewalk that's lined with a "No matter where you are from, we're glad you're our neighbor" yard sign on the left and a "Coexist" one to the right.

Given the stark uniformity of the other yards, I'm sure this woman was well-loved by her neighbors. Sebastian shoots a smug look over his shoulder, as if the liberal display proves his judgment in people is sound. The whole thing still feels off to me. As far as we know, the woman could've come across this place and is using it to lure people in for who knows what.

She walks up the stairs of the front porch and, pulling a key from her pocket, unlocks the door and opens it. All I can see is a long hallway from my spot at the bottom of the stairs. She steps inside, saying something I can't quite make out, and Sebastian follows her.

"Sebastian!"

He stops.

I plan on telling him he made his point and that getting killed isn't worth this nonsense. But he doesn't turn around. He just stands there.

The woman pokes her head around him. "You're welcome to join us. You will need to leave that bike and gun out here though. I won't have that shit in my house."

She pauses, as if expecting a response, but all I do is watch her, fuming. "Come on," she says to Sebastian. "I'll show you where you can get started."

She leads him deeper into the house and shuts the door behind them.

I consider getting on the bike and driving off. I'd turn around, after he has enough time to miss me. I resist the urge. There's too much of a chance that the sound of the engine disappearing in the distance will relieve him. No. I will drag him kicking and screaming to Miami if that's what it takes. I'm getting us through this. He'll thank me on the other side.

I listen, peer around at the land of middle-class success, and wait for a scream or a suspicious sound that would require me to rush inside. I pace back and forth in case the woman is working with a sniper in a neighboring house to pick me off. I know the slow movement won't prevent even a novice shooter from getting me, but it helps quell the panic rising from the thought that after all we survived, we are going to die quietly in the suburbs.

The first sound that comes out is banging. It's coming from the back of the house. A steady sound. I hide the bike as best I can on the side of the house behind some overgrown shrubs and hurry toward it.

I follow it to a back patio that's littered with strange, anamorphic sculptures and plants. On the other side of sliding glass doors, Sebastian stands with a rusting hammer and sheet of plywood. He places it against the inside of the door, obscuring himself, and the hammering starts again.

Boarding up a house for an old woman is innocuous in itself. Still, she's survived a long time in a very rough world without it. There's no way she's this unscathed by merely enjoying her life and pretending nothing's happening. There's more to her, and if I remain outside, then whenever that other foot falls, I'll be too late.

There's space under the back porch, beneath the stairs, that is a far better place to store the bike than the shrubs. I head back up front and grab the bike. When I return, the woman is standing on the back porch with a water bottle in her hand. "Thirsty?"

I eye her. Sebastian continues hammering inside. "I'm good."

"It's sealed. I figured you wouldn't drink anything that wasn't." She tosses it to me, and I nearly drop the bike grabbing it. "I wouldn't leave that thing out in the open, especially once the sun goes down. After dark, drifters and squatters can come out to play."

She's smiling, but her eyes are unfocused. A slight and steady unease I know all too well.

"We won't be here by dark." My gaze doesn't waver.

"There's plenty of hammering to be done. I have more than one if you want to help."

"The bike and gun stay with me."

"You're welcome to store them in the shed for safe keeping." She motions her head behind me to a small red shed that has vines and flowers painted on it. The door is secured with a big padlock.

"And who has the key to that lock?" I bet someone else has a copy who will take the bike and supplies after we get comfortable inside.

"Two keys. One is somewhere in New York in my husband's pocket if the White leaves bodies and keys. The other is right here." She takes a key off a ring of many and tosses it to me.

I watch it drop in the grass.

"Suit yourself. I'm gonna check on your better half." She walks down the stairs past me and heads to the front door now that the back is completely boarded up.

I wait for her to disappear around the house before moving the bike. The bottom of the stairs flanks it on either side, concealing it from everyone who isn't directly beneath the porch.

Time passes. The hammering continues. Sebastian's arm must be getting tired. I eye the water. Aquafina. My mouth is so dry that my tongue sticks to its roof. I open it and, even though the seal didn't appear to break until I did it, I inspect it for glue or any other signs of tampering. I come up empty, and after sniffing it for one last precaution, I take a greedy gulp. Then another. The relief is instant. I stop myself there and cap it so I can have the rest later. I collect the key from the grass and pocket it before walking around to the front of the house where the sound of Sebastian's hammering has relocated.

The thin curtains that cover the windows, which run the length of the front porch, let me see Sebastian within, placing board after board, blocking off the house from the outside world. Occasionally, he stops and takes a drink from a glass that is most certainly not previously sealed. I'm so busy making sure his actions do not indicate he was somehow poisoned or drugged that I barely notice the woman come out with a glass full of yellow liquid.

"It's lemonade, not piss." She walks down the steps and turns so she can watch Sebastian work.

I don't feel the need to validate the statement with a response.

Another minute or so goes by before she asks, "So, what happened?"

I keep my eyes forward, on Sebastian, but I make sure her figure remains in my periphery. "What do you mean?"

"Well, I don't think that blade your male caller has would be able to cut through the tension between you two, and it seems like it was there before I showed up."

I disregard her question and ask one of my own. "Why board up the house now?"

"Ah, a good, old-fashioned, quid pro quo, Clarice," she says in what has to be the worst Anthony Hopkins impersonation I've ever heard. "Well, I'm tired of the bunker, and I would like to enjoy my house and everything my husband and I amassed in our lives before it all gets taken away."

"Bunker?"

"My husband, George, was a survivalist. I had my yoga and meditation and what have you, and he had that. We both coped in our own ways after having an empty nest when our daughters went to college." She pauses to sip her lemonade before continuing. "You can only imagine my frustration when all that money and time he poured into the damn thing paid off."

Sebastian watches us with curiosity before covering the last window on the first floor.

"Where are they?" I ask.

"I don't know if you ever watched *The Silence of the Lambs*, son, but it's my turn to ask a question. That's how this thing works. So go."

"On what?"

"What happened between you two?"

I almost lie. Make up some elaborate hoax to see if she will buy it. But trying to keep a fake story straight sounds exhausting, and I will hopefully never see her again once Sebastian finishes up. So, I try to streamline the truth. "We grew up across the street from one another. Our parents were friends, so naturally, we were best friends. Then lovers. I got a scholarship to Trinity. He got a waiting job at this local restaurant, and we got an apartment together nearby. Then, I fucked it up, and the White hit. And now he's dragging his feet when we finally have a chance in Miami."

That catches her attention. "You got the radio message as well?"

I can't tell if I'm relieved that it wasn't just a local trick or concerned about how far the radio message reached. All those people rushing to Miami, vying for limited spots on those planes with even more limited resources is going to be nothing short of a shit show. I try to not think about it now and return to the woman. "We did. Where are your husband and daughters now?"

She clears her throat. "Well, the girls were stranded in New York when it happened. They were attending NYU, so it wasn't like they needed a car. Their apartment was in the heart of the riots. This was right after the Flight 112 hijacking, and we didn't want to put them on a plane. My husband, in his infinite wisdom, decided he was going to go get them. Too dangerous for me to go. I would stay put with the supplies locked in the bunker, and he'd be back. The cell towers were still up and running then. The girls stopped answering their phones the day he left. He barely got into the city when rioters ran him off the road. They took everything except the clothes on his back and the phone in its case on his belt."

She stops then and takes another sip of her lemonade. "They beat him close to death. He called me when he came to. Eyes swollen close to shut.

Leg broken. I tried to get a car, but it didn't work out. He managed to drag himself to an abandoned warehouse. He spoke to me on the phone as the White took him."

The mangled corpse of a man we passed in Pennsylvania comes to mind. Legs and arms bent in the wrong directions. We couldn't tell if he jumped from a tall, nearby building or was pummeled to death. We hoped for the former. I put my hand in my pocket and trace the shape of his crippled body into my thigh with the bulb of the pin. The fabric catches on the dotted scabs. The only thing I can think to say is "I'm sorry."

"First floor is done," says Sebastian from the doorway. He's standing too far within for me to see him from this angle.

She swallows hard. "Upstairs is next. The rest of the wood is to the right of the stairwell up there."

I try to listen for him and not get too distracted, but I have to ask, "What did your husband say?"

"Quid pro quo. Your turn. How'd you shit the bed with my handy man?"

I don't know why it all comes out so easily, as if it's a confession I've been holding in for years and need to say aloud in the hope of absolution, but it does. "I was finishing my degree, and he, well, he was doing what he always does. Taking it easy. Going with the flow. Figuring it out as he goes. I was the egotistical, money-hungry asshole. I just . . . wanted so much, I guess. I wanted better everything than either of us had growing up. We both did at some point, but, anyway, he was happy where we were. And I could already see myself getting comfortable with him. Complacent. Slowly all those big dreams started seeming like they weren't really needed. And that, well, it scared the shit out of me."

My vision blurs. I wipe away the tears.

The echoes of Sebastian's hammering float down from upstairs.

"So what happened?"

"I told him I couldn't settle for where we were. I told him I had big plans for my life, and I couldn't stay in that apartment or Connecticut and rot like our parents did before us, just scraping by. I told him when I graduated in a few months and our lease was up, I was leaving. I wanted him to come with me, but I knew he'd never leave our friends and would probably resent me if he did, and that I'd just end up hating him if I stayed. Then, hell, within a few days, the White hit, and now . . ." I trail off, finally at a loss for words.

"It's eating you both alive from the inside out," she says.

"Yep . . . Anyway. What did your husband say?"

"That rhymed."

"It did," I say, unsure how else to answer. "Did he—"

"He didn't say much."

I look at her to see if she's joking. Her face looks stern for a change. "He described how it felt, pulling him in like a warm hug or something. He said 'Wow' and that was it. Like he was relieved. I remember those researchers screaming bloody murder in those recordings—who couldn't? I don't know if he forced himself to sound that way for my sake or if he somehow found peace in what was waiting for him in the White. But he sounded relieved. And I've wanted to leave this house hundreds of times since then, but I kept fearing that the second I did, our girls would show up. They might've been in college, but they're still my babies."

Images of the White swallowing a bloodied and bruised middle-aged man berate my mind along with the idea that someone other than the deranged White Standers took peace in the White. Questions of whether everyone experiences the same end in the White only worry me more. I'm so caught up in my head that I don't realize the woman has added an addendum until she repeats herself. "What's your name?"

"Alexander," I respond, more of an exhale than a statement as I try to pull my focus back to this conversation and the hammering inside.

"Alexander, no one knows what this thing is. When it reaches me, I hope I'm just as relieved as my husband, but maybe I'll be screaming in pain. I've taken comfort in being a God-fearing woman, but I'm not stupid enough to believe this thing is some reckoning or punishment. I do look forward to being with the love of my life again. And even my beautiful girls someday because I refuse to believe that thing got them. You two, however, have the person who means the most to you right beside you."

"Maybe it would've been different had I not—"

She downs the remainder of her lemonade and tosses it thoughtlessly behind her. It shatters in the yard. "First of all, I wasn't finished talking, and I don't very much care for interrupters. Second, what you did or were planning to do before the White matters about as much as that cup. It's here. The world appears to be ending, and you're luckier than most. So please try not to be so pedantically miserable, okay?"

My knee-jerk reaction is to deny it. I'm not trying to be miserable. I just am. I feel like there is a difference, but as a minute passes, I can't find it. Maybe she's not altogether wrong.

"You hear me?" She elbows me.

"Loud and clear." I smile for what feels like the first time in ages. "So, why didn't that survivalist husband of yours board up your house before he left?"

"He was going to, but there wasn't much point until he got back with the girls. Why board up everything but the front door? It would just attract more passersby. Plus, I was technically fine in the bunker. But I have been listening to the radio and figured out generally when it'll reach here. A few thrill seekers track its pace. I was just going to enjoy my house tonight and chance it. Then, I came across you two and figured we could help each other out."

The hammering stops and the sound is soon replaced with heavy footsteps on stairs. "Isn't it going to be hard to see in there with all the light blocked out?"

She flashes a playful smile. "You'll see."

"All done," Sebastian says when he reaches the porch. He glances between us. I don't know if it is something in the air or a look on my face, but he can tell something more than small talk has transpired between us. "I left the last board by the front door like you asked."

"Good," the woman—Debbie—says, clapping her hands together. "Come with me, Rambo. You gotta put the work in, too, if you are going to reap the benefits I have in store for us."

If she has as much gasoline as she claims, then information won't be the only worthwhile part of this detour. As hard as it is to admit, I think I trust her. I follow her around the other side of the house to something large and square that's tucked between two overgrown shrubs and covered in a blue tarp that has bricks on top of it to weigh it down. She gestures for me to uncover it, and I do so to reveal a generator that is encased in a steel wire cage that is bolted to a cement slab.

Sebastian looks around us at it. "You've had a generator this whole time?"

"Your powers of observation are impeccable," Debbie says.

"Why haven't you used it?" I ask.

"Because I couldn't use a hammer—and should someone break in and I left the bunker, I would've been defenseless. And if the girls make it here, I don't want them to find my body or someone else waiting for them. But the White will be here tomorrow, and I just want to listen to some records, get drunk, and take a proper bath. Which brings me to your contribution." She reaches behind the shrub to a metal box on the side of the house. After flipping some switches within, she unlocks the cage and changes more switches on the generator. "Now take that handle," she instructs me, pointing to it, "and pull. It's the starter cord."

I make sure we are still the only people in sight. I lean the gun against the side of the house, grip the handle, and pull with all my might. A little sputter. I get better footing and do it again with the same result. What little muscle I had in my arm has long since been curbed by malnutrition. I don't know how Sebastian managed to do all that hammering.

"I can try," he offers.

"No can do," says Debbie. "We all work at my house to earn gas and food."

I pull back once more, this time, practically throwing all my weight into it and stumbling as I do it.

The generator coughs and hacks and comes to life. Debbie starts around the side of the house to the front door. We both follow her, and once Sebastian is ahead of me, I strap the gun back over my shoulder.

We just get inside when the lights come on. Debbie must've had every light switch turned on because the whole entryway with stark white walls and dark wood floors lights up. I'm so used to the only light source being the sun, a flashlight, or a candle that seeing all those golden bulbs bloom before us might as well be magic. They sparkle in Sebastian's hazel eyes as he admires them.

Debbie walks in from another room, beaming. "Aren't you glad you helped me out? Now, food and water are in the basement. Not everything is going to work with the generator, but we can microwave a dinner. I have enough jugs of water that you can bathe in the tub in the guest room. You are welcome to stay the night or, of course, take what you can carry and leave. The gasoline is stored in the bunker. Either way, I just ask that when you do, you take that final board out with you and nail the front door shut."

"How will you get out in the morning if we go now and nail it shut from the outside?" Sebastian asks.

She looks disappointed, like he asked a question with a painfully obvious answer. "I'm staying here."

"You're going to kill yourself?" I blurt out.

"A captain goes down with her ship. I've lived a long life, and I'm ready to see my husband again. And we all know I'm not making it far outside of this house."

"But," starts Sebastian.

"Look. This isn't a topic for discussion. I've made up my mind a while ago. I have enough bolts on my front door that should keep us safe tonight. I guess you can keep the bike and gun inside tonight as a precaution as long as you keep them the hell away from me. So, what will it be?"

Sebastian breathes in, about to say something.

I think of her advice. Of being lucky enough to still have Sebastian. Of our fight. Of everything we've been through and how, as much as I want to get on the road and drive directly to Miami, this may be the last reprieve we get before facing whatever is waiting for us there to get on those planes.

"We are going to stay," I tell her.

Sebastian turns to me, not hiding his surprise.

I pretend I don't see him, but his softened expression is a nice change of pace.

"Great." Debbie claps her hands together. A period on the conversation. "Come help me with the wine. We aren't going to have a sober end-of-the-world dinner party."

II

We all select whatever catches our fancy from the storage room in the bunker that is lined with shelves that hold all sorts of canned and dried goods. Sebastian goes for the instant Jambalaya. We both grab some beef jerky. For some reason canned yams and couscous sound great to me. Debbie selects the wine, and while I have been trying to keep away from any booze to stay sharp, I accept a glass to sip.

We sit in the dining room, our strange, microwaved feast steaming around us. Debbie declares that we can only discuss the times from before the White. Once we stuff our faces enough to keep the nagging hunger at bay, we trade stories. I forgot how nice the old rituals of a dinner around a table feel. I also forgot how nice warm food that wasn't hastily heated over a fire tastes.

Once we finish dinner, Debbie leads us into a family room toward the back of the house. She sits near the record player and switches records from a massive case behind her so she can enjoy her favorite songs from each album. Everything from Billie Holiday to Neil Young. I worry the sound is going to attract people, but after listening near the boarded-up window by the couch for the better part of an hour, I relax. Perhaps those who already picked over the other houses are farther south now. She gets Sebastian to dance with her to Skeeter Davis's "Once Upon a Time."

When Sebastian goes to change out the record, he drops the needle, and "The End of the World" starts playing. Debbie laughs hysterically, and when Sebastian goes to change it, she stops him. They say something to one another in a whisper. Then, Sebastian walks over to where I'm sitting. He extends his hand to me.

I eye him suspiciously for a moment before taking it. We sway together. I don't think we ever slow danced before. Neither of us neared the dance floor at prom. We spent most of the night outside on the patio of the venue, hiding from our dates, the McCluskey twins, and passing a cigarette back and forth while we watched everyone inside.

I picture us back there. Moving beneath party streamers and a disco ball. His big eyes and baby face staring back at me. Long before either of us held anything but love for each other and—

Crash!

Something loud shatters outside. I pull away from Sebastian, looking around wildly for the source. Debbie bumps into the record player and Skeeter Davis keeps repeating "world" until she pulls the needle from the record.

Silence consumes the house.

"The back porch." She points toward the kitchen.

I grab my rifle, and heart hammering, wine climbing up my throat, I charge into the kitchen. The back door and boarded-up window above the sink are still intact. I attempt to pull back a corner of the one at the window to peer out, but Sebastian has the board secured well to the wood trimming around the window.

I turn to go out of the kitchen and around to the front door, but Debbie blocks the way. "It could be a racoon or a squirrel. Those fuckers love knocking over my ceramic planters. Front door is still fine. Let's leave it. Come on."

We return to the family room. I sniff for the smell of fire in case they try to burn us out, but after a few minutes, I have to stop because I'm feeling lightheaded. Once another fifteen minutes pass without incident, I'm able to breathe normally again. Debbie grabs a Prince album, but when she plays it, she turns down the volume. I reposition myself in an armchair that gives me a decent view of the hallway to the front of the house and make myself breathe. We attempt to return to the festivities. However, the spell that kept away worries of the White and the world outside this room is broken.

When Debbie begins nodding off, we call it a night. She shows us to the guest room, and with jugs of water from the bunker, we fill the tub in the connected bathroom and heat up the last few gallons with an instant tea kettle.

We both stare at the steaming water. I say, "If you want to go first, I can take the second one."

I turn to leave, but he grabs my arm. Turns me around. There is a look in his eyes I haven't seen in a long time. A playful hunger. He kisses me. I kiss him back. I wrap my arms around his waist and pull his body close to me. I can feel him getting hard.

Every kiss and touch as we undress is both familiar and foreign as we relearn each other's bodies. All the sharp angles and muscles and bones from scavenging. His hands run across my thighs, and the speckled carnage there, but beyond a hitch in his breath, he leaves them be. I'm too caught up in the moment for the shame to reach me.

I step into the tub and pull him in with me. I grab the bar of soap and run it down his rocky spine. He kisses me. Takes some coconut-scented shampoo from a shelf next to the tub and runs his fingers through my hair. We wash each other clean, and then, soaking wet, I lead him to the bedroom.

After we've exhausted ourselves, he lays his head on my chest, and I twirl a lock of his hair between my finger and thumb. Neither of us say a word. He falls asleep, and I continue playing with his hair long after it dries. I wish we could lie here forever. That the White wouldn't be here tomorrow. That we could abandon everything, since I told him I was going to leave him until we entered this house, in the dirty bathwater and live out an odd existence here with Debbie. Wendy and the Lost Boys.

But we can't. The White will swallow this house and Debbie and every other poor asshole who gets in its way. We have to keep going. Keep fighting until we get to the equator. Once there, maybe we can say the words that neither of us dared to say tonight. Then, we can rebuild what I demolished and try to enjoy what's left of our lives.

Even after the generator runs out of gas and the electricity cuts off, I keep an ear out for intruders. I imagine us there, in some cabin in the mountains, on the other side of the doubtless roadblocks we will face on our way to Ecuador.

PART FOUR

FUCK

I

In the morning, I check the perimeter with the rifle in hand before refilling the generator. Shoeprints of at least two different sizes flatten the dewy grass around the house. I believe I stayed on the stone path yesterday, but I can't remember if Sebastian or Debbie did.

On the back porch, I find a ceramic pot in pieces on the floor. A turtle with the world on its back, shattered. The dirt within spreads out like black water on the light wood. I pick up whatever plant that is clearly floundering in the cool fall air and stuff it into another pot that's shaped like a frog. The White will probably destroy it as it passes through, but something about the sight of those roots, reaching out into the air for something to cling to, seems too pitiful to leave alone.

I report my findings to Debbie when I reach the front porch. Sebastian is inside, preparing breakfast. I survey the neighborhood around us as if the potential bandits will duck too slowly around a corner, and I will catch them. "Seems like someone was trying to see what was going on. The dew is undisturbed though, so the tracks are from sometime yesterday or last night. That doesn't mean they can't come back, though."

Debbie rocks on one of the two chairs on the porch. She shrugs. "If someone gets past the plywood, I'll flee, wine in hand, to the bunker."

Sebastian comes out of the house with three steaming mugs balanced in his hands. The smell is instantly recognizable, but I haven't had it in so long, I can hardly believe it. Coffee, along with booze and tobacco, was among the first items to become scarce during the shortages.

"Is that—"

"With powdered cream." Sebastian presents me with a mug. His eyes are alight with excitement. We were both caffeine addicts before the White.

I loop the rifle over my shoulder and take it. The smell is intoxicating. Head pounding from last night's drinking, I can't think of anything better. I look over at Debbie. "You're amazing."

"Thank my husband. I was always a tea drinker. He made sure to have plenty of coffee for his bunker. Can't survive the end of the world uncaffeinated." Debbie accepts her mug, which appears to be some kind of dark tea, from Sebastian and thanks him.

I take a sip. The bitter, familiar taste floods my mouth. I close my eyes and enjoy the moment, like I'm in some demented Folgers Coffee commercial.

I give Sebastian the other rocking chair and stand beside him. We all silently stare out at the street. It's already colored in the sanitizing light of the White, which has overtaken the sky to the north. An overexposed photo of abandoned suburbia.

Early on, when I first realized I had feelings for Sebastian, I pictured us in some neighborhood like this. White picket fence. Golden retriever. A couple of kids. I didn't even want kids, and I wanted to live in a city, but something about that image of that middle-class American dream stuck with me. The possibilities of how we'd spend our lives together were endless then.

"I assume you're planning on taking I-77 and then I-95 down to Miami?" Debbie asks.

"Yep." I make myself sip the coffee to savor it.

"I'd tread lightly near Charlotte." She doesn't look away from the street.

"We don't plan on doing more than pass through there on the highway," Sebastian tells her.

"Just watch yourselves. A few days ago, I ran into a girl. She was coming up north from there to her parents in Virginia. She said Charlotte was a ghost town, and the few people she saw there were clearing out the highway to the north with plow trucks. She didn't stop when they tried to wave her down because she had some sense, but it seemed like they were planning something."

"I'd understand clearing the road to the south to be able to drive out of the city, but why to the north?" I say, more thinking aloud than really asking.

"Not to be a pessimist, but I can't imagine it's a good thing."

I agree.

Strange.

She finishes her mug and tosses it off the porch. It shatters in the road.

I roll my eyes at her.

"Try it. It's fun," she says.

I'm not thinking of my mug. I'm considering how, unlike up north, where the ever-encroaching White created chaos that, while bad in its own right, was relatively spontaneous, these southern cities had more time to organize and do who knows what while they waited for oblivion to reach them.

I down the rest of my coffee and, if only to fight off the thought that everyone with sense in Charlotte went south to Miami, I draw the mug back and throw it. It breaks on the blacktop. The curved handle is all that remains intact like the severed half of a snake. One of Medusa's stone locks.

Debbie looks expectantly at me. I have to admit it. "It's fun."

Sebastian's mug joins the fate of the others, and we eat breakfast and get ready to go. We pack as much food, water, and gasoline as we can hold on the bike. We can always trade what we can't take with us on the plane. I top off the generator and rejoin them on the porch. The last plywood board saved for the front door is leaned against the house. Sebastian holds the nails in one hand and the hammer in the other.

"You're sure about this?" Sebastian asks for probably the tenth time. I know he's not asking about nailing the door shut—at least not exclusively.

"Positive." She smiles. It doesn't seem forced. She seems ready. "Thanks for keeping a woman in her prime company before the world ends. Now shut me in. I have wine to drink and music to enjoy."

I make eye contact with her over Sebastian's shoulder and mouth, "Thank you."

"I can't tell you how much we both appreciate you," Sebastian says.

She hugs him. "Good luck. The both of you."

As Sebastian nails the plywood over the door, I wonder what'll happen when the White overtakes the house. Will it pull it apart like a tornado? Slip in through cracks and vents to fill the place with a toxic mist? If Debbie retreats to the bunker, will she be safe as long as she doesn't open the steel door? A research group in Canada attempted to test whether underground nuclear shelters could withstand the White, but all cellular and radio communication cut off after the White passed over them.

Whenever or however Debbie goes, I hope it's painless. More so, while I doubt there is anything waiting for us after this life other than an unconscious expanse of oblivion, I hope, if only as a random memory as her mind shuts down, Debbie gets to be with her husband at the end.

II

As we near Charlotte, two facts become ever more apparent: One. We are burning through gas fast. Two. Something is very wrong here. The first only makes me more concerned about the second. I could chalk up the gas mileage to the added weight or Debbie's gasoline supply being old. There is, however, a much more plausible explanation, and, thinking back, clues are littered down I-77. I scraped the bottom of the bike fleeing that gas station. I assumed the worsening miles per gallon afterward were due to the pull of the White. I don't remember the bike leaking anywhere, but regardless, the bike isn't running right.

Despite the cold wind buffeting my face, sweat forms on my forehead in beads that streak into my hair. I should stop. But the girl Debbie spoke to was right about something strange happening in Charlotte. The highways are clear. All the vehicles that were presumably abandoned in traffic jams are pushed to either side of the road. Puncture marks are visible where a plow must've pushed them aside. The path is not only large enough for a car, but also a tank or a semi-truck. The fumes of gasoline from pierced gas tanks permeate the air, and I'm left with the question of what these survivors are planning.

Once we get past the city, we can assess the damage. We'll be too exposed on these open highways, and I have no intention of sticking around to see what the hell these people are doing.

I speed up. The bike seems to take more time to accelerate than usual. I try to remember the standard I'm comparing it to in order to see if my anxiety is just spiraling. No. It's typically faster than this. It had more power yesterday.

Fuck.

I take even, deep breaths through my nostrils. My hands are going numb, which must be from how hard I'm gripping the handle, not oxygen deprivation. I loosen my grip.

Sebastian stirs. He lifts his resting head from my back and calls into my ear over the wind, "What are you doing?"

"Just making up for lost time." I shoot past yet another unencumbered exit.

The weight on the bike shifts to the right. He's looking over my shoulder at the dashboard. I want to lean in front of him to block it, but it'll send the bike toppling over. I lean left and ask, "What?"

"Where the hell is the gas going?" While Sebastian may not know a Harley from a Honda, we've been riding with a gasoline focus long enough for him to know what is and isn't typical.

"We'll have to see once we get past Charlotte." I rush under an overpass and darkness descends for a second before the light returns.

"We should stop now," he hollers.

He wasn't awake to see how unsettling this place is. "I will after Charlotte. Trust me."

"Just pull over so we can make sure driving farther doesn't mess shit up more." The sharpness is back in his voice from before we got to Debbie's house. Last night was a temporary truce, not an end-all solution to our problems. He locked the bedroom door again.

I can't tell if I did something wrong since we departed or if the temporary cease-fire was just that—temporary. Anger boils to the surface faster than Debbie's instant tea pot. I still manage to hold back a remark about how he knows nothing about motorcycles. I do, however, pretend I can't hear him over the wind. "What?"

"Pull over." Not a question. A demand.

I speed up the bike. "What?"

"Just fucking pull over."

I'm about to respond—with what I'm not entirely sure, but I know it won't be kind—when he screams out in surprise.

I glance over my shoulder and see black smoke shooting out the exhaust pipe.

Fuck.

I slow down and stop under another underpass to give us a little cover. Even after I get off the bike, I still feel the shaky, uneven movement of riding down the highway—or at least that's what I tell myself is the source. I have the kickstand up before Sebastian steps onto the road. I don't immediately inspect it, though. I walk away from what I presume is the mangled corpse of our only means of transportation and peer out at the cleared road heading north.

As soon as I thought the bike was acting up, my mind returned to Philip. A flash of him in the garage, elbow deep in that old Harley, rushes back to me from a closet in my mind, where I boxed him up years ago and he only returned to me when we neared the White at that gas station. He let me watch him work as long as I didn't talk or touch anything. After a while, he turned down Nirvana and walked me through what he was doing.

I don't want to think about him. I told enough kids in high school that I was an only child that I almost believed it. Only Sebastian and older kids who had long since graduated school remembered him. But I'll need to return to that garage if I'm going to figure out what the hell is going on with this bike.

I grab the pin in my pocket and twirl it between my pointer finger and thumb. We don't have the time to get lost in the woods. Not here with whatever is happening in Charlotte. Most places we pass through leave behind a story of what happened in the wake of the White. Smudged fingerprints on the glass of a screen door. This is different. It's being cultivated for something.

I stab the pin into my thigh. I breathe in deeply as the jolt of pain hits me. I swirl the pin into the wound, relishing the hurt. Then, I pull it out. Leave it there in my pocket. Turn around to face Sebastian with what I hope is a look somewhere close to resolution.

Sebastian circles the bike in search of issues. "Doesn't appear to be leaking."

"Here, let me take a look." I wave him off. Heat radiates from the exhaust pipe and makes me sweat more as I inspect the bike. No glaring issues stick out, and the scrape on the bottom is superficial. I run through the symptoms in my mind. Poor fuel economy. Sluggish acceleration. Black smoke.

I go back to the endless evenings in the garage with Philip. I block out the distant screams of my mother and father arguing inside and Philip, long hair, thin frame, leaning over the bike. I think of the old Harley he got from the junkyard that seemed to have every issue under the sun. He spent a while on the engine, but that didn't seem right. I remember him holding out an air filter that looked like it swallowed a bird's nest. That could account for the problems. Could also be a bad carburetor. Another memory, tweezers pulling charred gunk from the machine, comes back to me. I hope for the air filter. A much easier fix. Either way, we'll need tools to find out.

"See anything?" Sebastian asks.

I explain the prospects to him. "I suggest we try to make it down the highway until we get to a smaller town. We can find an auto shop there so that we can see what's going on."

"Will we need parts to fix it?"

"We won't know until we take a look." I think I hear something in the distance. I whip my head around, but I don't see anyone approaching. We should get going.

"Will a little shop have what we need?"

I already know where he's going with this, and I don't like it. "Come on. Let's go. We'll reassess once I can take a look." I get on the bike.

Sebastian remains standing. "I want to avoid cities as much as you do, but we don't want to get stranded on the road. Plus, Charlotte is a different city than New York. Who knows, maybe there is still a mechanic in the area. We could trad—"

"What? You heard what your friend Debbie said. They're doing something here. Look around." My voice rises as my irritation mounts. It's like he wants to just pick the opposite of whatever I say, and I can already tell this is leading right back around to our disagreement from before about threading friendship bracelets with every person we come across until they put a bullet in the back of our skulls.

Sebastian tucks a few loose strands of hair behind his left ear. "Given the option, I'd rather avoid it. And if you weren't set on Miami, I'd agree. But I don't want to deal with the possibility of being stranded without the bike, any transportation, or anyone to trade with to continue on our way."

"Deal with it or with me?" I ask, but I know the answer. The truth of the matter—which is that Sebastian is right, that I'd probably lose my damn mind if we became stranded, that I will be putting us both in more danger in Charlotte for Miami, and that we don't have a choice—takes the fight out of me. "Let's go then. I want to be out of the city before the White nears."

Sebastian narrows his eyes.

"What?"

"Great idea," he says in a deadpan.

I recoil. "What do you want from m—"

The growling of an engine, getting louder by the second, stops me mid-sentence. The underpass fills with the sound. Not coming at us from either direction, but overhead. I wait for whatever vehicle is on the road above to pass, but it stays put. I hop off the bike and wheel it over to the wall of the underpass, waving for Sebastian to follow me. His annoyance, like mine, has been sapped in the face of a potential threat. He joins me.

The engine cuts off and silence falls upon us. Sebastian watches the concrete above us. I split my attention between the road to the north and south.

A rush of static, and then a man says, "I'm not seeing anything coming or going. Over."

"You must have missed them then. I'm telling you. Two people on a bike. They just came through there. Over," says another man's voice.

Click, and then the first man says, "Mona, block off the road before Carson. If Jeremy is right, they should be there in another minute or so. I'm heading that way. Over."

"I'm on it. Over," she says.

The static cuts off and all that remains is wind rushing through the underpass.

"Fuck," Sebastian breathes out, summing up all the thoughts bombarding my mind.

This is bad.

Very bad.

They're going to block us from getting through, and it's not like we can double back and go around the city with the bike on its last leg. Not with the White at our heels.

After the vehicle drives off, I breathe out, and in my body's rush for new oxygen, I cough and begin gagging. Some mixture of coffee and wine and food from the night before crawls up my throat, and I'm just barely able to shut my mouth and swallow it back down while breathing through my nose.

Sebastian rubs my back, but he doesn't look much better himself. The color has drained from his face. "What do you think they want?"

I know what he's thinking. The same thing I am. New York. There were blockades throughout the city. As we were trying to get past one of them, we watched a group of men box in a van. They dragged the whole family from the vehicle. A man, woman, and toddler. They tossed them onto the blacktop like they were sacks of flour. The mother's screams were so loud, so desperate, that they were forever seared into my memory. Them and the accompanying gunshots as we sped off.

Bang.

Bang.

Bang.

We came across a man on a spit over a fire later that day. Food was scarce. But not that scarce. The people around him were wearing sunhats and plastic grass skirts with tiki torches around them, laughing and drinking like they were at some white-washed office party luau. Sick bastards giving into their darkest desires in the aftermath of civilization.

Just thinking of that bubbling, black flesh makes bile shoot back up my throat. I swallow hard one more time. Lingering on what happened or what could happen isn't going to get us to Miami. I try to put on a brave face for both our sakes. "Doesn't matter. We will be gone before we find out. If we take it slow, we should be able to drive into the city and find a place to regroup before finding a shop. If it's just the air filter, we can clean it out and aim for an exit farther south. With the White getting close, I doubt we'll be on their minds for long."

Sebastian opens his mouth to say something, perhaps to ask if it isn't the air filter, but he stops himself. "Let's go."

I wheel the bike to the middle of the road. I can see the next exit from here, and those people already think we are way past it, so we'll be able to at least slip into the city unnoticed. What's waiting for us within is what I'm worried about.

I get on the bike and white-knuckle the handlebars. Sebastian gets on behind me without a word. I turn the key, and the bike stalls.

Fuck.

I try again, and this time, it thankfully starts.

I breathe out, but it doesn't relax the tension in my chest.

All I can see in the side mirror is the White billowing behind us. Even with the miles we put under our belts earlier today, it'll be here by dawn tomorrow. It keeps getting faster. A ticking bomb that's counting down as we scramble to fix the bike and avoid whatever the hell those people are doing in the city.

My thoughts are consumed by how we could meet our end at the hands of these drivers, spliced together with the memory of Philip's waxy skin in his open casket, the woman's screams in New York, Debbie dancing in her house as the White swallows her, and the knowledge that the endless fights Sebastian and I have along the road never seem to be resolved, just interrupted. A supercut of chaos that could end on this highway.

The stone pillars of the underpass feel like they are closing in on us. I take off as easy as I can. I try to think of some way to halt the onslaught of mounting dread that is infecting my bloodstream, but nothing comes to mind. The only thing that will lessen the panic is getting through Charlotte and out the other side before the White hits. Because this is just a bump in the road on our way to Miami. No different from the gas station and the countless other setbacks we've faced so far.

I repeat that to myself as I drive off the exit and into the city.

LIFE
IN THE
CITY

I

The panic attacks became worse after Philip died. The nerves were there from as far back as I can remember. I was so worked up after my mother left me at daycare the first time that I vomited. My hands shook so bad during class presentations in middle school that I could barely read my flash cards. I often fled to the bathroom during Sunday church services because I felt like I was suffocating in that sea of packed pews. Still, I managed to get through most days without completely crumbling.

Then, a spotlight focused on my existence after Philip's death. Every look and action were given special attention because my big brother died. I wasn't eating enough food at dinner. I looked too tired in first period. I was worrying too much about an upcoming chemistry test. I seemed detached at track practice. I needed to let out the grief or focus on the positives or just keep doing the best I could.

Cutting helped numb the urge to set myself on fire. A nightly ritual. After my mother and father turned in for the night, I got the sandwich bag of sharp objects and wound care from a loose floorboard under my bed. Sanitized the knife. Reopened one of the scabbing wounds on my thighs. Doused it with rubbing alcohol. Savored the pain. Dressed it with ointment and a band-aid or two. Focused on the aching hurt until I fell asleep.

It wasn't just the pain. It was the process. The methodical nature of it that I have largely lost on the road as I attempt to recapture those blissful moments of oblivion with pin pricks. Driving into Charlotte, I have no time for anything to calm my shallow breaths and pounding heart. No time for anything except taking in the city rising around us. Because this isn't our city; it's theirs.

Townhouses with tall trees growing up from the small patches of grass between the sidewalk and street whiz past us. All the front doors are shut, but I notice a few broken windows. Vehicles are turned over on sidewalks, wrapped around trees, and pressed against buildings—everywhere except the road. This looks like a main road the people with radios use.

One of their vehicles could appear from a side street any second. The motorcycle engine running hard could draw them right to us. I suddenly feel we are seconds away from disaster. I wanted to get farther into the city before regrouping, but we have no idea what we are driving into. Sebastian has to feel it, too, because he points toward a parking garage opening on the other side of the street. I make a U-turn, drive past the broken parking barrier, and duck inside.

I turn left and almost run right into a pile of cars that's pushed to the outside walls of the garage. I cut right, tires screeching, and slow to a stop in the cleared path. I turn off the engine. Let my eyes adjust to the darkness. A lot of the open walls that are supposed to let in sunlight along the first floor are blocked by the cars. Similar to the roads, someone cleared a path.

"What the hell?" I put up the kickstand. Clearing a road makes sense, even in the wrong direction, for travel. A random parking garage though? I don't like this.

The smell hits me then, above the gasoline from the smashed cars. A boy's high school locker room, except the slight, but somehow worse, reprieve of Axe Body Spray among the body odor and sweat is replaced with rot, piss, and shit. I turn away, gagging, but the smell is waiting for me there as well. I lift the collar of my shirt over my nose and blink through my watering eyes.

Sebastian hides his nose in the crook of his elbow. "Jesus, the—"

"Help!" A frantic, guttural scream comes from somewhere above us.

I look to the cleared path that disappears around the corner to the second floor of the parking garage. I blindly hold out my hands for the rifle while I watch the path, waiting for someone to appear from the shadows.

Sebastian hands me the rifle. The dangling strap hits against my legs as the gun shakes in my trembling hands.

More voices join the first.

All from different sources.

"Up here!"

"Hurry!"

"Help us!"

Others just yell without words.

A symphony of fear and desperation that doesn't seem to be getting any closer.

I realize then that this isn't just a random parking garage. This must be connected to whatever the hell those people with the radios are doing. We didn't find a quiet place to regroup. We walked right into the lion's den. And we need to leave. Now.

"Get on. The bike," I say, but it comes out in an unsteady whisper as I try to catch my breath.

"What?" Sebastian says over the screams.

I force air into my lungs. "We need to go!" I tear my gaze from the path and scramble onto the bike.

Sebastian stands there. Frozen.

I thrust the rifle into his hands. "Sebastian. Come on."

I don't know if it's the panic in my voice or the force with which I give him the rifle, but he stirs. He loops the rifle strap over his shoulder and climbs on the bike. I turn the key. The accompanying reverberation of the engine never comes. It stalls.

No.

Not now.

I try again.

Nothing.

Again.

Fucking nothing.

I hear an engine then. But it isn't from the bike. It's in the distance.

We hop off the bike. We need to get out of here. I start toward the entrance. But the sound is coming from that direction. I double back, searching for another way out of here. Scrambling. No different from a cockroach fleeing the beam of a flashlight. No emergency exit or side door in sight. Just a wall of cars and the path up to where those people are screaming. Standing, I try the key in the ignition.

The vehicle draws closer, seemingly taunting the useless sputters that erupt from the bike as I continue trying to get it to start.

"Alexander," Sebastian says, somewhere behind me.

"We have to get out." I keep trying it. A thousand needles prick my fingers that are going numb from the lack of oxygen.

I shut my eyes and try to take a deep breath and think of a way out of here and not of how lightheaded I feel. My lungs refuse to carry any more of this putrid air.

Oh god. I'm going to pass out here and lead whoever is in that vehicle right to Sebastian. Our voices will join the screams above in who knows what horror awaits us. A lookout probably saw me drive into the garage. That's why this vehicle is coming.

"Over here. Hurry. There is room behind this car." Sebastian's voice pulls me back to the moment. He stands in a gap between a van and a Beetle farther down the wall of cars. Looks like there is just enough room to get the bike through the space and apparently behind the Beetle, where Sebastian is shining his flashlight.

I don't want to stay in this garage. I don't want to find out what the hell is happening here. I don't even know if I can make it the ten feet without falling over.

The vehicle will be here any minute though. It must be coming down the main road, and I can't imagine it has any other destination but this garage.

I concentrate on Sebastian, and despite my darkening vision, I push the bike forward and move my legs so that, even if I pass out, I'll be close enough for him to drag me the rest of the way. Sebastian backs up behind the hood of the Beetle to make room for me. I lead the bike to the gap and somehow make it there.

I turn around when I reach it and pull the bike through by the handlebars. They clear the space. I assume the rest is fine and peer at the entrance. The bike stops moving. The bags and supplies fastened to the middle of the bike catch on the sides. I pull harder, but I'm too dizzy to put any strength into it. I reach wildly for the bands holding the bags in place. A truck pulls into the parking garage. The headlights turn, nearing where I stand uselessly with the bike.

Then, I'm falling, and only after I land on Sebastian do I realize he pulled me down. I shift off him and roll to the ground. I can't breathe. The light passes over the cars. Exhaust muddies the air as the truck rounds the corner. The driver must not have noticed the bike. The people screaming above fall silent. The immediate danger has passed. So why isn't the tightness in my chest passing? Why can't I fucking breathe?

Sebastian says something above me. He pulls my head into his lap. Rubs my chest. Pushing my hair away from my face, he whispers, "It'll pass. Just breathe with me. Come on. In. Out."

I focus on his hand rubbing my chest. Picture it releasing the death grip on my throat and lungs. I follow his instructions. Everything else in the world fades away.

In.

Out.

Eventually, my body relearns this basic process.

I sit up and turn to Sebastian. "Thank you."

He nods.

Before college, therapy, and medication, he was the only person who could talk me down. Countless nights in high school, even before we realized we were attracted to one another, we lay side by side on his bedroom floor, and he made every unbearable aspect of my life in the wake of Philip's death seem manageable.

Before I told Sebastian I wanted to break up, I spent many late nights and early mornings selfishly wondering how I would make it without him. Even then, with a stabilizing prescription cocktail and a bright future ahead of me, I couldn't imagine doing it alone. I realized, beyond the different paths I saw our lives heading, it wasn't fair to saddle him with me.

Because he took care of me, long after he wanted to do it. The least I can do now is keep it together. I grab the pin, find the most recent wound, and jam the pin back into it. The pain stops me from spiraling further. Maybe I don't need the process. Maybe I can get by on the pain. It only needs to work until Miami.

I can't keep falling backward into panic attacks and our old dynamics. I have to keep in mind why we are doing this. We aren't in his bedroom or Miami. We are in this garage. The driver of the truck shut off the engine. We need to go before one of those desperate people on the next level rats us out or more people show up. I get to my feet. Take a breath. Wheel the bike back out into the cleared path.

Sebastian stops, his attention on the next level. I know what he's thinking, and I quickly explain, "Whatever is going on up there has nothing to do with us. Come on."

Sebastian doesn't give any indication whether my assessment is correct. In a painfully tired voice, he says, "Let's get moving."

II

Sebastian stands by the window, peeking through the blinds at the road. The pale light of the ever-nearing White comes through in lines that break up the shadows of the office. A black-and-white photo from a home printer that's running low on ink. The image spliced with negative space.

Two blocks from the garage, we came upon a one-floor insurance office building that was ransacked but is still in decent shape. Probably because most of what filled the building is relatively useless. Computers, filing cabinets, nineties furniture with faded geometric fabrics, and slogans like "Better safe than sorry!" and "We have your back!" plastered on the walls. We shut ourselves in the largest back office that, according to the wooden name plate on the desk, belonged to K. McNeil, to regroup.

Only then, out of immediate danger for the first time since we drove into Charlotte, do we have a second to process what the hell we just experienced in that garage.

"Those people," Sebastian says. "They have to be keeping them against their will. And that smell. How long do you think they were up there?"

Those people aren't high on my list of priorities. The bike isn't working. The White is getting close. And there were many voices on that radio working to collect people for who knows what. I want to sever the garage from my memory and focus on getting the hell out of here. I get up from the leather chair at the desk, still feeling the post-panic-attack exhaustion, and walk over to the window. "I don't know."

He watches me carefully. "They were screaming for help."

Apparently, my suspicions in the garage were correct. We can barely help ourselves, much less random strangers. But he isn't going to accept that answer. "Maybe they're criminals? Law enforcement could be trying to keep the city from turning into New York?"

"The truck was plain. Not a police car. Plus, some of those voices sounded young. Like kids."

His eyes remain trained on me. Unsure of what reaction he does or doesn't want to see, I try a neutral expression. "They could also be working with the people in the vehicles. Luring us in until the truck returned." Sebastian glares at me, so I try to level with him. "We are in no condition to save anyone. See that light. It'll be here by dawn. If we—"

"Everyone trapped up there will die. Every voice we heard."

"They're going to die either way!" I hate how angry I'm getting. But we've already had this conversation. "And we will too unless we fix this bike and get out of here."

He throws his hands up in exasperation. "How are we any different from them?"

"We have a bike and have enough luck to not be in that parking garage. That's it. If we somehow get the bike working and go up there, we're going to get killed. They're going to throw us from the bike and kill one another until they break it or someone else takes it. I get it. Not everyone is a monster. There are some Debbie's in this world. There are also awful, selfish people. The White doesn't care which one we are."

"I'm not an idiot." Sebastian walks over to the bike that is parked at the door. "I know that. I'm just having a hard time letting all those people die. Can I be a human for a minute and care about something other than ourselves?"

Whatever I was expecting from him, it wasn't that. The implication is clear. I'm a selfish asshole. He's reaching into one of the bags on the side of the bike. I thumb the wound on my thigh, picking off the dried blood through the fabric in my pocket, to level myself. "We need to find an auto shop. Get what we need to fix the bike and get the hell out of here," I say. He continues searching the bike, like he doesn't hear me. "What are you looking for?"

"Water." He turns around, holding the bottle out before opening it and taking a drink. He waves his hand like he's a king. "Continue."

My frustration surges, and all I want to do is grab him and shake some sense into him, but then it just makes me feel empty. A flash fire, leaving charred remains in its wake. I don't know at what point on this road that we fell so comfortably into these roles of him glaring at me and me rolling my eyes at him that the dynamic has become second nature. The grooves are too deep to figure out when the first cut was made.

I point out the window. "The White is following us. Every minute you spend mourning strangers, it continues its pace. You can be human, but I feel we keep having the same conversation and getting nowhere. Then we start it over. So, what is the real problem? Because I don't want to fight with you every step of the way, and I can't tell if you just like casting me as the heartless bad guy so you can be the pure optimist, or if it's something else."

I regret asking the question the moment it leaves my lips. We both know the answer. The source of every fight we've had on the road.

Sebastian opens his mouth and thinks better of it. He still doesn't hate me enough to state the obvious. He takes another sip of water that lasts a lifetime. "If there aren't planes when we get to Miami. If they're already gone. Ruined. Or who knows what, then we are going to die."

I refuse to even entertain the idea that we'll surrender to the White on a Miami beach. "And whether or not we helped those people in the garage isn't going to matter."

Sebastian shakes his head. "Or it's the only thing that matters."

I don't even know where the hell to start with that. Out the window, the White isn't moving fast enough to get noticeably closer since I last looked outside, but it is. We don't have time to continue with some philosophical debate all day. "Before we do or don't do anything, we need to fix the bike."

Sebastian downs the rest of his water, crushes the plastic, and tosses it beside the desk. "Fine."

He fills a backpack with a few snacks and water bottles. I hope we won't be here long enough to need them. We move the leather chair and wheel the bike behind the desk. With a tarp over it, anyone who comes across the office will hopefully overlook it upon first glance. Keeping it with us will only slow down our search for a shop. Still, leaving behind the only constant we've had on the road besides each other, one that has carried us through so many calamities, feels like jumping out of a spiraling plane with no parachute.

I silently promise the bike we'll be back soon. Then, I unlatch the office window on the way out to give us another entrance should we need it. We head out in the opposite direction of the parking garage, sticking to side streets and alleyways that, unlike the cleared main roads, should keep us away from whatever those people are planning.

III

Even in small towns, we might run across someone migrating south or White Standers congregating to be eviscerated by the White. No one and nothing here. We pass a quiet block of apartments, and despite not spotting any movement on the ground or in the windows, I can't shake the feeling of being watched.

We continue past them to a gas station. A corner store. A bar. A massage parlor. I wish for the convenience of a smartphone or computer right now. A single search would give us an exact path to an auto shop. Instead, we continue wandering about, hoping to magically discover it.

One of the reasons we wanted to move to the city when we were young is because everything is supposed to be within walking distance—except, apparently, auto shops. I think back to all the places we lived and visited and try to think of where the shops were generally located. I supposed they were randomly smattered about most places. Near main roads but perhaps not exactly on them because of the space required to repair cars and park them before and after said repairs. Ideally, right where we're searching.

We're cutting across a parking lot in the back of some restaurant when the roar of an engine stops us in our tracks. We're out in the open. I search our surroundings for the closest thing to duck behind, and I spot a crunched van on the sidewalk across the lot.

"Over there," I say, running toward it. Sebastian hits the ground beside me mere seconds before the Jeep turns onto the street. I expect it to pass, but it's moving at a snail's pace. I inch more under the van and pull Sebastian along with me.

As the vehicle nears, I can make out the music over the engine. "Wouldn't It Be Nice" by The Beach Boys. Someone in the vehicle whistles along to the beat. They don't stop near the van. They keep going, slow and steady, down the street. Going nowhere in no particular rush.

Sebastian's face shares my confusion as he helps me to my feet. Then, it comes to me.

"Patrolling."

We press forward. The longer we are out here, the more likely we are to run into one of those people. And the light of the White continues brightening everything as it approaches.

More streets. Vacant buildings. Thirty minutes after the Jeep drives past, the silence of the city is interrupted. An engine. Close. We rush over to a dumpster at the mouth of an alleyway and duck behind it. My heartbeat pounds in my ears, making it hard to hear where the damn thing is coming from and verify if the driver saw us.

There is just enough space between the brick building and the side of the dumpster for me to see the road. A white truck appears from the west where we were heading. No music. A bearded man scans the area.

"That's the guy from the garage," Sebastian says. His whole head is practically sticking out in the open.

"Get back!"

He leans closer to me. "Relax. He didn't see me."

I check the road from my vantage point, and it's thankfully clear. I wish it made me feel better, but the frequency of the rounds is troubling. "Do you think one of those people upstairs tipped them off to us?"

"What? No. Why?" Sebastian gets to his feet.

I follow him. "I'd be surprised if they've been keeping up rounds like this. No way they have that much gasoline to burn through."

He doesn't respond. We start toward the street. Then, the engine returns. Fast.

I nearly fall over in my rush to grab Sebastian and get us both back behind the dumpster, but I manage it. The engine stays at the same volume. Close. I check my opening.

The white truck idles, right at the damn entrance of the alley; so close that I can see the rear fender is smashed from some sort of accident. The hiss of static, and the man says something into his radio I can't make out.

"Where is h—" Sebastian starts.

I shush him.

The engine shuts off.

I motion to Sebastian that he's right there. I look behind us. The alleyway is clear. All the doorways littered down the patchy blacktop are shut. If we try to run for it and the man has even the slightest aim, we'll be easy pickings.

I check again. The man gets out of the truck and walks around the hood. He's tall and stocky. His flannel shirt is tight around his biceps, and his face is largely obscured by a brown beard that is far thicker than the hair on his head. I can't make out for sure whether he's armed.

I ready the rifle and push air in and out of my nostrils because if I freeze up now, we're goners. I don't think about the man I shot in the leg at that gas station or the look on his face as we drove away. I think of that family pulled from their vehicle and murdered. I think of Miami.

"And where the hell do you think you are going, huh?" the man says.

I try to count his steps on gravel. My deep breaths are making it hard to hear. I try to slow them. I'll hyperventilate at this rate. I aim the rifle over Sebastian so that when the man comes around the corner, I can pull the trigger.

Then, a woman screams. "Please!"

A baby cries.

I lower the rifle and check the opening.

The man stands over a van that's on the sidewalk. "Don't you worry. I'm not going to hurt you or the little one. We must get you back home. The White will be here soon."

"No. No. We won't go back there. Please. Let us be." The voice and baby's shrieks seem to come from within the van. I think it's from the cabin until the man reaches under the vehicle and yanks the woman out from under it.

She's young. Probably late teens. Gaunt with matted black hair and dirt-covered clothes. The baby is wrapped in a clean yellow towel in her arms.

Over her pleas and the baby's cries, the man says, "We need all the Lord's soldiers. Come on."

The man pulls her to her feet, and once she's upright, the woman elbows him in the face and takes off down the alleyway, right toward us.

The man quickly recovers. He pulls a magnum from his back pocket and aims it at her. "Stop or I'll shoot."

Sebastian grabs my arm.

We have to help her, he mouths, pointing to the rifle.

The scene runs through my mind. Us popping up from behind the dumpster. Him changing his aim and blowing a hole through Sebastian's head. No. We could, however, try to surprise him when he comes around the dumpster after her and—

Bang.

The shot echoes through the alleyway. The woman falls, her head just in sight of us. The baby's screams are muffled beneath her. Face twisted in pain, she focuses on us. "Oh god. Please help us!"

Sebastian goes to get up. I pull him back down with as much might as I can muster in my free hand. The man could shoot either one of us on sight. Despite the air moving through my nostrils, the lightheadedness returns. I hang on to Sebastian. Pretend his hand is back on my chest. Hear his voice.

In.

Out.

"God has a different plan for you." The man is close. "You shall atone for your sins, and your sacrifice shall save this city and His true followers from our Lord's wrath. There is no need to be afraid. This is His plan."

The woman tears her gaze toward the alleyway. She screams, eclipsing that of her baby, and, within an instant, she's dragged out of sight.

Tears streak Sebastian's face. In a harsh whisper, he says, "What are you doing? We have to—"

I drop the rifle and clasp my hand over his mouth. I whisper, "If she was shot, we can't help her now."

Sebastian tries to pull away from me. I hold him there. He fights to free himself, but I don't let go until the engine starts and the truck drives off with the woman and baby inside.

Sebastian pulls free. "What is wrong with you? We could've helped her."

"He would've shot us dead if we tried." I get to my feet. My vision darkens for a second as blood rushes to my head. Sebastian trudges down the alleyway toward the street. He passes a black puddle that collects the woman's blood from wherever she was shot. I follow behind him. "Where are you going?"

"After them." Sebastian doesn't look back as he cuts right out of the alleyway in the direction the truck must've gone.

I hurry after him. "Are you crazy?"

He doesn't answer me. He jogs down the small path remaining between the vehicles and building fronts. Whether he could come across another driver making their rounds, a lookout, or who knows what doesn't seem nearly as important to him as catching up to the truck, which makes a left at the end of the street.

I strap the rifle over my shoulder and stay alert as I continue after him. He's far enough ahead though that when he cuts left, I'm still only halfway down the block. I try to speed up. Regulate my breathing as I go.

In.

What's he thinking?

Out.

He can't be thinking.

Just as I round the corner, I spot the truck, turning right. The man in the truck seems to be maintaining his same relaxed pace, moving in the opposite direction of the parking garage. It doesn't make sense. Something's wrong. Sebastian's right on his heels. Maybe the man saw him in his rearview mirror, and he's leading us into a trap.

I chase them another block, closing the gap to only thirty feet or so.

"Stop before you get us both killed," I say in some combination of a whisper and a shout that I hope reaches Sebastian and not the driver.

He makes a right without acknowledging a word I say. I keep after him. He slows to a stop in front of a row of shrubs that are still lush with dark-green leaves. I catch up to him as he kneels behind them, peeking inside the greenery.

"What the hell are you—"

"*Shh!*" He yanks me down to his level and, moving a branch, directs me to look through the opening. Across the street, the truck pulls into a gravel lot. There are tire tracks in the light rocks that lead to what looks like the loading dock of a massive steel warehouse. The truck keeps to them with an ease that must come from regular trips to this location until he reaches the building. Knowing the driver had a destination in mind and wasn't going somewhere to ambush us is a small relief.

I pull Sebastian's hand away, returning the shrub to a mass of branches and leaves. "Have you lost your mind?"

He ignores me, reaching for the opening with his free hand. I grab that one as well, and he whips around to face me, seething. "I'm not just going to watch this guy kill a woman and her child. It's two versus one. We can take him."

His eyes are wild in a way I've never seen. "Take him? What are you talking about? You want me to kill this guy? You aren't thinking straight."

"We don't have to kill him. We could just . . . take his gun and truck. Help that woman and her baby. And those other people. Hell, we could take the truck south." His conviction leaves his voice as he speaks. I don't mention how that man would be on the radio before we even have a chance to subdue him or that the road south is still very much crowded with abandoned vehicles that we can't navigate with a bulky old white truck. He seems to put that together on his own. "We can't just watch her get murdered and do nothing."

The sadness washing over him guts me. "I was going to shoot him as soon as he passed the dumpster. But he didn't. It all happened so fast. We didn't let anything happen. He did something horrible, and we couldn't help her. That's it."

"No. There's still time. Has to be."

The truck engine cuts off, and rattling, grinding metal takes its place. Sebastian pulls back the branches of the shrub. The man, with the baby on his hip, stands before one of the massive garage doors that is being pushed open by two people inside. As they lift the door, the light outside catches them, and I see two men, dressed as plainly as the driver. Behind them is a cattle car. Even after the arms reach out from the rusted slats, desperately searching for freedom, and pleas and angered threats fill the air, it takes a minute for my mind to put together all the pieces. Maybe because I didn't want it to.

The cleared path to the north. The parking garage. The smell of human waste and rot. The people being held against their will. The man's assurance of how this woman will sacrifice herself and her baby to save the city. The cattle cars full of people. How many could they fit in the parking garage and this warehouse? How many more were out there throughout the city?

"They're going to drive them into the White," Sebastian says, voice shaking. "Those lunatics are going to drive them all into the White."

Sebastian's free hand finds mine. I squeeze it.

I want to say no. Pretend he is somehow conflating things because there is no way that could be true, but I can't. Between the White Standers and the people in New York, we've seen how the White can drive people mad.

In the early months of the White, there were seemingly endless, infuriating discussions from radical religious groups of how this was no different from the universal flood in Genesis. A cleansing of the sinful. Protests to keep criminals locked in prisons near the Canadian border as opposed to transporting them south. Bombings of nonprofit healthcare providers and LGBTQIA centers that promote sinful activities. Assassinations of leftist politicians. All in the name of saving our country from being engulfed by the White.

I'm sure if there had been more time and more organization among those groups, what's happening in Charlotte would've happened countrywide. I can picture it now. Buses of everyone who doesn't fit their standards being launched into Canada to appease their God.

The anger returns. I have little doubt that if we were living in Charlotte, we'd be in one of those cattle cars. All those people. I wish then that we were invincible. That this was some action film where we could come running around the shrub and take down who knows how many people inside without so much as a scratch and let all those poor people free. But we aren't superheroes. We are just two gay men with slightly better circumstances than the people in those cattle cars.

Another engine nears. A beige van drives into the lot. A man and woman get out of the van and walk toward the truck, where the bearded man, who must've handed the baby to someone inside, is pulling the bleeding woman from his vehicle.

"Bless you, you've found her," the woman says, clapping her hands. She's beaming from cheek to cheek, making her round face look like it's on the verge of popping. "The last of our wandering daughters returned before we take sacrament." She, like the others, is dressed casually. Jeans and a sweater. A part of me wishes they were in those idiotic white robes with their faces painted. Somehow, I think that would make this less awful, but I don't know why.

"The patrolling. They were looking for her," Sebastian says.

Among others—the woman said she was the last of their daughters to be found. Some of their prisoners must've gotten out. If they've caught everyone, then maybe the patrols will stop. With the White drawing close, they'll have to organize.

"They seem to be converging here," I tell Sebastian. As if to provide more support to my assumption, another truck comes around the corner and pulls into the gravel. "We should go."

Sebastian lets the branches fall. I can see the gears turning in his mind, and I prepare myself for some grand plan.

"We've been wandering about for the better part of two hours though. We can't keep going around in circles."

I'm not sure where he is going with this. I'm just glad he hasn't suggested trying a suicide run at the warehouse. "We'll find one. With them being busy here, we'll have more time to find an auto shop."

"If we found a local though. One who knows the city. They could lead us right to a shop."

And there it is. He didn't change his mind at all. He wants to let those people out under the guise of them giving us directions. "Are you seeing what I'm seeing? How do you expect us to get directions from someone in that warehouse with all these drivers flooding the place? We aren't—"

"I never said we'd try to talk to one of these prisoners," he says, cutting me off. "They're all meeting here, which means the parking garage is probably—"

"No," I say. My turn to cut him off. I'm too exhausted and disturbed by what we've learned to even be mad at him. "We can't. They could lie. There has to be someone guarding them. If the patrols have stopped, then we'll have plenty of time to find a shop on our own."

Sebastian doesn't respond. He just looks past me at the sky. I follow his gaze. The rolling clouds of the White are close, lighting up the city despite the dying afternoon sun. He waits a minute. Lets me take it all in before he says, "We haven't found a car shop yet, and soon the streets will be filling with those cattle cars. We might not be able to save them all. But we can probably save the ones in that parking garage. Get the directions for a shop. And get out of here sooner than we can randomly come across it. It's risky, but so is everything we do in this city while those people are here. We are as much helping ourselves as them."

My eyes don't leave the White. I don't like this plan. Not one bit. But all the reasons why we shouldn't do it don't seem nearly as persuasive as the ones for it. Furthermore, those reaching hands through the cattle car, that woman's smug look at finding their prisoner. My first and only priority is getting us out of this city in one piece. However, if we could help out some poor bastards along the way, I wouldn't be against it. As long as it doesn't put us in more danger. "We better get going then while they're still distracted."

Sebastian tries and fails to suppress a smile.

"What?"

"Nothing. Just glad to see you still have a heart somewhere in there." A playful tone. A flicker of what used to be and what could be again if we survive this mess.

"I still think this is a bad idea." I turn back the way we came before he can see me break a smile.

"There he is," Sebastian says. But he isn't running ahead. He walks beside me. For the first time in a long time, we're in this together.

I

"I'm not seeing anything." Sebastian lowers his binoculars. We crouch behind a discarded truck across the street from the parking garage. The cement square towers overhead. The openings in the top-floor walls are less obstructed by cleared-away cars than the first. Still, from this angle, it's hard to make out much that isn't near the edge.

"With a runaway, and the White so near, you'd think they'd have someone to watch these cattle trailers around the clock." I see something out of the corner of my eye. I cut my gaze toward it, but there doesn't seem to be anything there.

"If we spot anyone, I know a good place to hide." Sebastian forces a smile.

Come on, there is no use visiting him if you are just going to mope. Think of how he feels. He wants to see his little brother happy. Come on, Alex, give me a smile.

My mother's words return to me now. She stood over me, demonstrating the fake smile she mastered long before I took my first breath. The juvenile detention center, an impenetrable rectangle of brick and black-tinted windows, overtook the sky behind her. Philip had been there for fourteen days. My mother had gone the previous Sunday. Apparently, he hadn't said a word to her except to ask after me.

Standing in the parking lot, I parted my lips and showed her my teeth.

My mother maintained her smile. Through her teeth, she said, *It'll have to do,* and dragged me toward the entrance.

I became better at fitting that mask of complacency over whatever I felt. Although, on the road, I've lost practice. I must look as tired and scared as I feel. Sebastian's probably worried about another inopportune panic attack. I offer a lipless smirk. The fear is still there, but something else has joined it. Before, we were cornered and surprised. Helpless. Now, we have a plan. A risky one, but one that could get us out of here and back on track for Miami. My heart is still trying to bust though my ribcage, but knowing that we have a means to survive this mess keeps my breathing steady. I prepare the rifle. "Let's do this before anyone gets back then."

We hurry across the street and through the entrance. This time, I notice the scrape marks at the top of the pass and the snapped bolts that held a clearance sign. The cattle trailer must've demolished it on its way through. Inside, the awful smell returns. I watch the bend ahead to the next level and listen for the sound of an engine. If a car comes through, it could blow through us before I have the chance to make a shot.

Footsteps on pavement and our shared heaving are all I hear. We only slow down when we reach the bend. I peer around the corner. The road ahead is clear. I wave on Sebastian, and we go up to the next level. I tell myself I'm having trouble catching my breath because we're running. That's all.

The second level has more light than the first. It shoots through the openings in the walls in fat beams, hitting the nearest stone support pillars and casting sporadic shadows across the level. Among them, I parse out a few vehicles pushed out of the path or parked in the far corners. No headlights or drivers in sight. Toward the back of the level, near the turn to the third floor, I spot the massive steel rectangle. A cattle trailer for transporting horses or cows. Or people.

We rush toward it. Between the flashes of light around the pillars, the smell of unwashed bodies, the screams that start when one of them spots us, and the nagging feeling that headlights will appear behind us and run us over, I feel like I'm in some awful nightmare. I keep hoping I'll wake up back in Debbie's guest room, but we near the cattle car with no such luck.

Voices from within interrupt and overlap each other.

"Help us!"

"Dear God, get us out of—"

"We have kids in here."

"Quick, before they get back."

Outstretched, skeletal arms wave and reach for us. When we stop at the back doors, gaunt faces and bulging, panicked eyes float in the shadows. Who knows how long those sick fucks have been keeping these people imprisoned without food or water.

Through heavy breaths, I urge, "Please, be quiet. We don't want them hearing us."

It comes out too airy to be audible.

"We are here to help," Sebastian calls out. "We need to speak with you though. Please. Someone who knows the city. We don't have much time."

He picks up the silver padlock on the door. Shakes it. It's locked.

More calls for help. Others shush people. Someone's crying. I check the turns to the first and third levels. No headlights. But they could be back any second. Stomach acid shoots up my throat, and I swallow it back down.

"Hush up!" a gravelly voice orders, making the others fall silent. An old man with sharp features and a patchy white beard steps toward the nearest opening. I wait for him to speak, but he stares at us expectantly.

"We're looking for a car shop," Sebastian says. "Our bike needs repairs. We know what those people are doing, and if you point us in the right direction, we will get you out."

"Horse shit," comes a man's voice with a thick southern accent inside. "They will leave us in the dust after they get what they want."

The old man turns to whoever said it, and the voice doesn't return. He looks back at us. "What's wrong with the bike?"

Sebastian turns to me. I take another breath. The man's milky eyes focus on me. My mind goes blank. "Not sure. Ah. Just need tools to troubleshoot more than anything. Tools."

The man considers us. Then, after presumably realizing he has nothing left to lose, he says, "Marco's should have it."

"Where's that?" Sebastian pulls the man's attention back to him.

"Get us out, and he'll tell you." A woman appears at his side. Her skin clings desperately to her bones. Her coarse black hair, which is streaked with white strands, wraps around her head like an abandoned bird's nest.

"We don't have anything to break the lock," Sebastian explains. "Would Marco's have something to remove it?"

The man raises his eyebrows as if he's surprised that he didn't think of that. "I'd imagine they'd have bolt cutters."

The woman looks at something behind us, and I jump before turning to face it. Nothing. Still, she focuses on it. Past us at the nothingness. The man holds himself like we came across him on the street before the White and asked him for directions. For a moment, he made me forget the horrors these people experienced. Enough to drive some of them mad. I try not to think about it or how this parking garage will probably be guarded by the time we find Marco's and fix the bike.

However, a truck or van or anything could turn the corner, and we will be in there with them. We need to get moving. "Okay. How can we get there?"

"And what guarantee do we have that you'll come back?" the woman asks, like she read my mind. I can feel the heat of shame on my cheeks, and I hope the shadows hide it.

I'm still wracking my brain for an answer when Sebastian says, "Because we aren't like them. You get us to the garage, and we'll come back for you." He raises the machete and stabs the tire near the wheel. Air hisses from the wound.

I resist the urge to ask him what the fuck he thinks he's doing. The drivers thought they captured everyone who got out, and a busted tire is going to raise some alarm bells.

"I say we let them rot like the rest of us." The woman grins.

"Enough!" the old man says. She whispers something under her breath I can't make out as she steps back. "You'll have to be quick. They plan on shipping us out in the next hour or so."

"Who's driving?" Sebastian asks. He must be wondering the same thing I am—who is willing to sacrifice themselves to the White for such an insane cause.

"Repenters. Whoever is running this has them screwed up enough to think they can absolve themselves from their past sins or some horse shit like that by offing themselves and the rest of us and saving God's flock." His voice rises as he speaks, and I can hear his loathing for these fuckers in his final words. The man composes himself. "Where you headed from here?"

"South," I say at the same time Sebastian says, "Miami."

The man turns back to me. "The radio call?" Before I can answer, he says, "Well, you are in luck. Get us out of here, and I can do you one better. I live a couple miles outside the city. Have a little puddle jumper. Seemed more fun than a Porsche when I retired. I probably have enough room to fly you two out of here."

Sebastian says something to him in response, but I miss it. A plane. Pass go and collect two hundred dollars right to Miami. Hell, depending on the fuel, we might not need the other planes in Miami. For the first time since the farmhouse, that glimmer of hope that we could make it through this reemerges.

The thought is so tempting.

A solution to the endless shit show that descended upon us since entering Charlotte.

No need to drive the rest of the way down.

We found a better option.

Too good to be true, especially coming from a man highly motivated to ensure our return for his salvation. I can't blame him. If the roles were reversed, I would say anything to free Sebastian and myself.

I do my best to take the crushing disappointment in stride. If we can fix the bike, we won't need anything else. The old man is speaking, but I don't catch it. "Sorry?"

He starts over. "Marco's isn't too far away . . ."

II

We just make it out of the parking garage and across the street when I hear an engine in the distance. We pick up the pace. Marco's is one block farther than our initial search radius, closer to the warehouse than I'd care to get. We do have the benefit of going right past the insurance office though. I have to admit that I'm excited to get the bike back. Without it, I've felt exposed. Naked.

I remember joking to Philip that the Harley he was working on was his girlfriend. He shook his head. *She's more than a flame. She's an appendage.*

I don't think I understood the sentiment until the phantom pains of the Kawasaki Vulcan's absence engulfed me as we wandered around the city.

I go to step out from a car we ducked behind, and Sebastian stops me. Another car passes by.

"Thanks," I tell him. I need to focus. We aren't out of here yet.

The vehicles increase in frequency, dispersing from the warehouse and whatever "sacrament" that woman mentioned. Each one we avoid serves as a reminder of how close we are to ending up in a cattle car. The drivers. The White. The bike. It all seems to be drawing near, and one misstep can result in our deaths.

Despite a few close calls, we make it back to the insurance office without being detected. In the office, I grab two water bottles and hand one to Sebastian. We stand there, shaken and exhausted, watching each other with the bike between us.

"What are you thinking about?" Sebastian asks.

"Get to the garage. Check the bike." I leave off the decision to be made after that point. There's too much that could happen in the meantime. We need to take this one step at a time.

Sebastian finishes off his bottle. Like before, he crushes it, but I can now see from where I stand that he doesn't throw it on the ground. There's a recycling bin by the desk he tosses it in. I almost laugh. I can't think of the last time we worried about where our trash went. The White eats it whether or not it's in the right bin. I'm about to say something to that effect when he speaks first. "We can probably fly to Miami in a matter of hours. Reach it before sunrise."

I search his face for some indication that this is sarcasm. No smirk or raised eyebrow contradicts the sincerity in his voice. "You believe him?"

"Why lie about it?"

"I can think of a few reasons." I finish the water bottle and throw it pointedly on the ground. The air in the office suddenly feels too stuffy to breathe. I open the window more for air.

"Is believing there could be a plane in Charlotte so different from believing there is one in Miami?" There it was again. That cutting tone. I had never heard it before that night. I went to Sebastian. He was watching TV. Tears in my eyes, I told him I couldn't do this anymore. That I had to leave because if I stayed and made us both miserable, I'd hate myself more than I did in that moment.

Sebastian didn't cry. His expression hardened. Voice sharpened. "Okay."

No questions. No heated words. No tears of sorrow. Just immediate acceptance that made me wonder if he'd felt the same and was relieved that I was the one who finally said something.

I wish I could say that I didn't understand why the animosity had returned so quickly, but we both knew the answer. We've each played our part in this delicate dance for a while. I didn't ask why he believed there was a plane in Charlotte as opposed to Miami. He didn't ask me why I wouldn't discuss our plan after fixing the bike.

Sebastian wants to return to them, regardless of whether the place is crawling with drivers. Keep his promise. I want to do the same, but not if it means dying in the process. I wonder if I should tell him that. I'm not sure if it matters. That cold *Okay*, and the memory of him stalling at the edge of the White at the gas station, makes me wonder if a plan with such bad odds is exactly why he wants to help them.

I keep it to myself. After all, there is no guarantee what we'll find at the garage, if anything, once we get the bike fixed. "Fair. I'm glad we are in agreement then. We should go. We are running out of time."

Sebastian watches something on the ground in the direction I threw the bottle. He doesn't look up. "We should go."

III

The wind picks up outside. I man the bike while Sebastian keeps a lookout as we move against the pull of it toward the auto shop. With the bike, there's no diving behind cars or bushes. Thankfully, the rush of vehicles slows. Hands around the handlebars, I feel better about our chances. Just a few more blocks. Then, if it is the filter—it has to be the filter—we'll be out of here.

Sebastian jogs to the next corner, and, making sure the coast is clear, waves me onward. We continue like this, only coming across one more truck when we are behind a row of shrubs, until we reach Marco's. The building stands in a paved lot on the corner of a block.

"Marco's" is printed on what was probably once white but is now a pale-yellow sign at the top of a pole that has old tires stacked at its base. The maroon paint that covers the cinder-block structure might've once drawn onlookers to the garage. Now, it looks like the muddled color of dried blood. The few glass windows that are not shattered on the two garage doors are cracked. All of which is covered in purple spray paint that asks, "What if the White is just the beginning?"

Sebastian gives me the all-clear signal from the intersection. I run as fast as my feet can take me, pushing the bike toward the front door that is also missing the glass in its window. Until we reach it, we are sitting ducks to any vehicle that drives by. I continue checking the roads to make sure the wind in my ears isn't obscuring the sound of an engine.

I resist the lingering question if my aching legs and shot nerves will feel better if I turn around and run toward the rolling clouds. I know it's the White trying to get into my mind. That's why Philip and the breakup and everything else is coming back to me. I hope it hasn't reached Sebastian yet, and if it has, the prospect of helping those people is keeping it at bay. We are so close to getting out of here.

Sebastian gets to the door first and holds it open for me. I push the bike inside. Once the bike is over the threshold, I pull the kickstand and grab my rifle. I know this could be a trap.

"What are you—" Sebastian starts, but I raise a finger to my lips to quiet him. The main room is small and dark with the only light coming in from a window in the door. I turn on my flashlight and press it to the barrel. A line of vinyl seats with stuffing coming out of nicks in the fabric line the wall to our right, ending in a door to the garage. A door ahead of us. Then, just a front desk to our left.

I rush around the desk. Nothing to find except an overturned cash register. I cut across the room to the other door and push it open. A cramped bathroom. Toilet and sink. I hurry through the door to the garage. All I smell is grease and metal. The room is lit from the White that seeps in through the broken squares of the garage door. There's a car without wheels in the center. A few stools. A steel door at the back of the building that's latched. Supplies line the walls with various, unmatching metal stands and cabinets.

"We're clear," I say to Sebastian, who stands behind me.

I don't realize until seeing his surprised look how quickly and manically I tore through the place. The dread of what might happen didn't overwhelm me. My stomach is settled and breathing steady. Nothing except a fire. An anger. Burning white hot. We've come too far. Survived too much to die in an auto shop in Charlotte. We're going to make it. We're going to escape the fucking White. The alternative isn't an option.

I strap the rifle back over my shoulder. "We should be able to get to the air filter with an Allen wrench. I say we start with that. If you want to get the bike, I'll find the wrench."

Sebastian goes back for the bike. I get to work. I rip open drawers and search through cabinets. A simple tool. That's all we need. The more it evades me, the more my anger mounts and the faster I search. Metal clinks and crashes as I work, and before I know it, I'm in my family's garage, where Philip made sure every tool had its rightful place.

It was after his funeral. A fit—that's what my mother called it. I went into the garage to get away from the mourners and fake monologues of how the good die young. The next thing I remember, I was demolishing Philip's sanctuary. Whipping drawers into walls and tipping over stands. It took my father and two of my uncles to pull me away.

I swallow the memory. This isn't about Philip, Sebastian and me, or anything before the White. This is about getting a part and getting out of here. The White must be infecting me more as it closes in on us, trying to pull me back to that place. Stop me from escaping the city. The very thought of it winning helps bring me back to the present.

Focus.

I work through another stand before finding a CRAFTSMAN hex key pack toward the back of a drawer. Sebastian has just put up the kickstand behind me. He trains the flashlight on the air filter cover. A metal dome with a single bolt at its center. Hands slick with sweat, I pull out a key and try it. I manage to slow the shaking enough to put it in the bolt and realize it's too small. Same with the next one up. I try the largest, but it's too big. My father reading *Goldilocks and the Three Bears* comes to mind. *This one is too little. This one is too big.* I try the next one back, and it's a perfect fit. *This one is just right!*

I spin the wrench around and around until the bolt releases enough for me to grab it with my fingers and work it the rest of the way out. I wipe the sweat that runs down my face. Dry my hand on my pants. Grab the dome and pull. It doesn't budge. Nothing else seems to be keeping it in place. Stuck. I pull it side to side with all my strength—my arm aching from getting Debbie's generator started—but it stays in place.

Sebastian minds the door as I work. I stand. I hold onto the handlebars to steady the bike and bring the heel of my boot down on the dome. It shifts. I aim another kick. It pops off and clanks to the ground. Rust corrodes the metal plate within. Three screws secure the filter in place. However, yellowed grass and brown leaves stick out from the sides.

"It's packed," I say, and the relief makes it almost come out as a laugh. The screws are a little harder to loosen, but I make quick work of them in my excitement. I pull it off, and sure enough, what looks like a mangled recycling bin is compacted in half of the filter. The other half is blackened and dirty. I dump the contents out. Run my fingers through the slats, sending soot, grass, leaves, and the rest tumbling to the ground.

I don't care about the way it darkens my fingers or the germs that crawl across my hands. This could be it. Just a filter standing between us and freedom. Once I clean it as best I can, I tap it on the ground to shake off what's left. Then, I pop it back on and, after screwing it in, reattach the cover.

With a prayer to all the old and new gods for a miracle, I mount the bike. I turn the key. It stalls.

Fuck.

I can feel Sebastian watching me, but I avoid his gaze.

This has to work.

I try again.

It stalls.

This can't be how we go.

Again.

But I'm not in Marco's garage. The undertow already has me back in my family's garage, sitting atop the Harley. My legs don't reach the floor. It was the summer before my growth spurt. Even our mother, who loathed motorcycles, came out to see the finished product. Philip was clean. Earned his GED. Worked on the bike all summer. He was going to bring it by Mr. Henderson's garage. Word about the bike had gotten around town, and Mr. Henderson said to show him it when he was finished. He might have a job for him. My mother was teary-eyed. My father had to give it to him, he finished what he started. I got to sit on it. Pretended to be Robin on the Batcycle.

He lifted me off the bike. Promised when he got another helmet, he'd take me around the block. Headed out for the auto shop. My mother broke into tears after he left, and for years, I wondered if she somehow knew what was going to happen. Only later, when I learned about his rocky road to sobriety, did I realize they were tears of joy. He was getting his life together.

The semi-truck driver wasn't drunk. He was a new father trying to save money for his twins. Went to bed a little too late. Got up a little too early. Wanted to wait on coffee until later in the day. He was almost back home. Mr. Henderson's shop was just off the highway. Less than a mile from our house. As Philip drove through the intersection, the driver blew through his red light. The helmet didn't save Philip.

It tore him open! Tore him open, Ron! I remember hearing my mother sob through the air-conditioning vent near my bed. They were in the basement, trying to collect themselves before they came up to my room, sat on the bottom of my bed, and told me he was gone.

There was no way life could be that random. That callous. There had to be a reason. At some point, when my admiration for Philip soured to anger at his abandonment, I told myself it was because he strayed too far off the path to ever recapture a normal life. After a senior told me about the break-ins and how his girlfriend showed up to work one day with a black eye, I was sure of it. He didn't follow the rules, and it caught up to him.

So, I got my act together. All A's in school. President of the National Honor Society. Treasurer of student council. Awards for community service. A scholarship to Trinity. Despite my family, my hometown, Philip, and every other roadblock, I was going to earn my happily ever after. The White wasn't going to ruin that. I didn't fight so hard for so long to die here. We have to make it. Because I have to fix the only mistake I've ever regretted. I have to save us.

Sebastian's arms are around me. "It's okay."

It's not okay. I can't breathe. I can't see through the tears. All I can do is try to endure the sobs that overtake me. Loss overwhelms every ounce of my being. Crumbled against the bike, I wonder if this was the only ending we were ever getting. Maybe my family was cursed, and I've dragged down Sebastian with me. "I'm sorry. I'm so sorry."

"We'll find another way." Sebastian rubs my back. But I can hear it in his voice, too. A distance he took to process that we are as good as dead.

I never even got on a motorcycle until after the White. We barely managed to drive around cars on the highway to Waterbury. Then, we came across a bike in the driveway of a one-story house. An old Kawasaki Vulcan 900 Classic. I pounded on the door to see if we could barter for it. The door was unlocked. We located the owner in the tub. The bathwater was red with blood. We found the keys on the kitchen counter. I thought in some strange world that Philip was looking out for us.

I curse Philip now. Because if he ever loved me, he would will this into existence. He would save us. It's the least he could do after he deserted me. Left me to stumble through life and ruin my relationship with the only man who ever really loved me.

"How do we check on the carburetor?" Sebastian says. He repeats himself. "Huh? Alexander?"

My face and hands prickle. They're numb. My throat will close soon, and I'll be even more useless to Sebastian than I am now. I fight my way back to his voice. Carburetor. "We'd need a replacement. I wouldn't even know where to start. That's why I hoped it was the fucking air filter."

Pathetic thing. I bring my hand back and hit the filter with all my might. The pain is instant, and for a moment, I try to focus on it. Use it as I had with the pin pricks to get by, but it just makes me sadder. A band-aid for a gunshot wound. An old trick that was just a distraction. Nothing else. A way of whittling myself down to survive.

I try the key one more time. Because I don't have anything else to lose, and the only thing worse than trying would be lying down and accepting our doom.

The engine sputters.

Catches.

Roars.

I look up at Sebastian to make sure I'm not imagining it. He's laughing.

He wraps his hands around me. The tears keep coming. The black smoke emitting from the exhaust pipe turns clear. I hold onto him. "We are going to get through this."

That's when I hear them. The hellhounds. The snarls of their engines. Tires on cement. We separate. A vehicle stops at the garage door, its headlights piercing the windows. I hear another one somewhere behind us. The headlights of a third light the office to our right.

We're surrounded.

IV

We fixed the bike. We were going to drive the hell out of here. With Debbie's supplies, we were going to make a quick journey to Miami. It was all in reach. Mere minutes from zooming off the exit and onto the highway.

And now?

We're trapped by those lunatics. They'll imprison us in one of those cattle cars. Not long enough to waste away. We'll be sent into the White. Presented to it on a platter to be devoured. An offering to their angry God.

The crushing reality of it leaves me at a loss.

It doesn't make sense.

We fixed the bike.

The worst is supposed to be behind us.

A car door slams shut.

Sebastian grabs my shoulder. "They're coming."

At least three cars and who knows how many people.

There are too many of them for mere coincidence. Had one of the patrol cars seen us, they wouldn't have waited for backup. I realize it then. Only the prisoners in the cattle car knew our destination. My first fear upon entering this shop was correct—it's a trap.

Those fuckers sold us out.

The fury that ignites at the realization of their betrayal grounds me. We aren't going to die here. I turn away from the light. Look for the best way out. We need to move. Before they have a chance to set up a perimeter. Garage door won't work. No power to raise it, and they'll have us before one of us lifts it open. Navigating the bike through the small office will be cumbersome. Behind us. The steel door.

I hop off the bike. Give Sebastian the handles. I grab the rifle and remove the safety. "I'm going to open the back door. Make sure we have a clear path. Then we are going to drive the fuck out here. Okay?"

Something like determination overtakes the fright on his pale face. "Okay."

"Come out now, with your hands up, and all will be forgiven," comes a woman's voice from the car parked out front.

I go to the door. Pull off the latch. With my hand on the doorknob, I pause and make sure Sebastian is behind me. He stands right at my heels with the idling bike.

I yank open the door and quickly return my hand to the trigger. Yellow light blinds me. Black spots cloud my vision. The white truck is parked ahead of us with its high beams on. The cabin appears empty. I step through the doorway, searching for the bearded man. Wind rushes around me. The left is clear. I'm turning right, and the next thing I know, the world is turning on its side.

The rifle fires, but the sound seems a mile away. I'm on the ground before the pain floods my head. My ear is ringing. The bearded man stands over me, knuckles red from where his fist connected with my skull. He's saying something. He pulls his magnum from his back pocket.

I don't know where the rifle went. It isn't in my hands. I try to lift my head to look for it, but the pain keeps me pinned to the cement. He aims the gun at me. A silver blade comes from the door, cuts through the air, and lodges itself deep into the man's arm. He falls back, blade still deep in his flesh, and drops the handgun.

I reach for it. The pain is so intense that I feel like I'm going to pass out. But I get a hold of it. I'm being lifted into the air. The world is spinning.

I fear I'm losing consciousness. Then, my feet are under me. My vision steadies on Sebastian, who is at my side.

His words are a garbled mass of sounds that slowly take shape. "Re ou kay? Are you okay?"

My head pounds, but knowing there are more of those lunatics coming for us helps me focus through the pain and dizziness. I cling to Sebastian to steady myself. "We have to go!"

He helps me back into the garage. A black silhouette fills the doorway of the office.

"You must atone for your sins," says the shadow.

I aim the handgun and shoot in that direction until I run out of bullets and Sebastian is pulling me back. The bike. I take one of the handlebars. He puts up the kickstand that he must've put down to help me. I run the bike toward the door. I only look back as we are going outside. Two people are running toward us.

Sebastian slams the door shut behind us. But we both know it will only delay them a few seconds. The bearded man reaches into the cabin of his truck. I get on the bike. Sebastian is right behind me, the rifle in one hand.

"Go!" he screams, grabbing onto me with his free hand.

I floor it.

The back tire squeals. The front of the bike lifts into the air.

For an awful moment, I fear it won't get traction before they catch us. That they'll yank us to the ground, and we'll be driven into the White within the hour. The next second, we are propelled forward. The bike shoots past the truck. Gunshots ring out. I cut the bike right and swerve around the building.

"Are you okay?" I scream to Sebastian, unable to look back to make sure a bullet didn't hit him.

"Yes. Drive!"

I steer the bike around two cars out front to the blacktop.

The wind whips in my face as we fly down the street and away from the White. Sebastian must've strapped the rifle over his shoulder because he wraps his arms around me. Something between a scream and a laugh escapes my throat. We are going to make it.

V

We're nearing an exit that promises to take us south to Columbia when Sebastian calls into my ear, over the wind, "Where are you going?"

"Getting us the hell out of here." I'm so elated to leave Charlotte and those sick fucks behind that I don't even think about why he asked a question with such an obvious answer.

I try to push everything else out of my mind. The gunshots. The blood. Just how close we came to being captured. My body still shakes with the shock of what we just survived, and my head feels like it is on the verge of splitting open, but we are only ten or eleven hours from Miami. That's all that matters now. We have enough gas and food to get there. I won't sleep until we reach it. Not until we're on a plane.

I maneuver the bike around the vehicles stopped near the exit. The drivers had no reason to clear the path in the opposite direction of the White. Sebastian says something as I find a path through them, but I don't hear more than the tail end of his sentence in my concentration. "What?"

"Pull over!"

I check the rearview mirror for smoke. Nothing. The engine sounds normal. Unable to find any other reason why we'd stop when we are almost out of this hell hole, I ask, "Why?"

"Pull. Over." The urgency of his words is so profound that I do as he asks without a second thought. I stop in the merging lane of the highway. I put up the kickstand, but I leave the engine on.

I turn to him. He's already off the bike, face flushed with anger.

"What's going on?" I ask.

"You were really going to leave those people to die, weren't you?"

It takes me a moment to put together what he's saying. I stopped worrying about them the second I heard the engines outside the auto shop. "They sold us out."

"You don't know that for sure." The words come so quickly that I wonder if he already anticipated my response and had his answer ready.

I get off the bike so I can properly face him. "Those drivers knew exactly where to find us."

"Maybe one of them noticed us along the way and trailed us until the others were in place." The frenzied look in his eyes returns. The bearded man's blood speckles his hair and face.

We've just gone through a lot, and while I already packed it away to deal with on the other side of our journey, he might not be able to do so as easily. It helps soothe my mounting frustration. "Maybe you're right. Either way, I'm sure they've connected the popped tire and us. It would be a suicide mission to go back now."

A vein in his forehead that I don't think I've ever seen before pulses at his temple. "Did you ever plan to go back to them?"

He looks disgusted with me.

I know then that here, on the highway, he plans to finally speak about what both of us avoided in the office. "Did you think that man had a plane, or was that just a convenient way for me to do what you wanted?"

"If we leave now, we might as well be dragging them into the White. How can you be okay with that?"

I can't believe what I'm hearing. "I'm not! I don't want to let them die. I think it's horrible. But joining them in the cattle cars because we walked right into another trap isn't going to do them or us any good." He isn't thinking straight. The White must have a hold on him. Calmer, I add, "The White has to be messing with you. We can't go back. We have to leave."

My words don't soften him. They only piss him off more. "Oh. So now I'm crazy? Great. I'm crazy for wanting to help people, even after it isn't convenient."

Here we are again, back to the start. And I'm too drained to pull back this time. Too mad to keep circling around it. "We both know this isn't about those people. No more than this is about that man at the gas station."

"No. It is. I won't be able to sleep without seeing those faces if we leave now and—"

"Just stop it!" I can't do this any longer.

"Stop what?" A dare. To address the tension that has followed us since I walked into the living room with tears in my eyes.

"Look. I'm sorry. I'm sorry. What else can I say? It's not like you even cared enough to ask a reason. Maybe because you were tired of carrying me on your back, and this was the easiest out. Me ending it. So that you could still be the good guy. So why don't we stop the charade, okay? I get it. I'm an awful piece of shit. I ruined us. I know nothing will ever change that. But I'm trying. I'm fucking trying. Don't you see I will regret it until the day I die? Why are you trying to twist the fucking knife in when we barely made it out of that auto shop." I'm crying too hard to see his face. He doesn't yell at me. He doesn't say a word. It makes it all worse. "Say something!"

"When did I say I wanted you to end it?" There isn't any anger. Only pain.

The question takes me aback. I don't know what response I expected, but it wasn't that. "You said 'okay' when I ended things. You didn't fight for us."

"I didn't know I had to. I didn't know it was some test." His voice shakes.

"I—"

"You'd already decided without ever telling me. You were resigned. What did you want from me? You wanted me to beg you to stay so you could resent me the rest of your life for settling?" I go to respond, but he doesn't let me. "I don't think anyone or anything will ever be enough for you. And for a while, I hoped I could be, but you made sure I knew that I wasn't."

I'm so confused that all I can say is, "What are you even talking about?"

"We were getting by. Our apartment wasn't anything special, but it was ours. I loved that place, and you acted like it was going to give you a cold. Never brought anyone by. Never put a single picture on the wall or bought a potted plant because this was just a placeholder until you could get a good job. You know how fucking soul sucking it is to be trying to make the best of things when you turned up your nose to everything?" He's crying now too, and as he rubs the tears, the blood smears in streaks on his face.

I think back to that time. The endless craft projects and random yard-sale finds. I thought he was just keeping himself busy after work. It wasn't that I was above it. I just didn't have the time. "I was busy. I was in school. Trying to get us that perfect life we always dreamed of. Remember that? We were going to have a big house. We weren't going to end up as bad off as our parents. We made a promise to each other. You forgot that along the way. And I knew if I stayed there, made you keep helping me pull myself together, you'd hate me. So, I did what you wanted. I ended it. Whether or not you realize it, you wanted me to do it."

"I didn't forget. I grew up. Wild dreams are a great way to survive in a small town full of people going nowhere. We got out. We could support ourselves—even without fancy jobs. It was never going to be enough. And that has nothing to do with me. Ever since Philip died, it's like—"

"Leave him out of this!" The words come out as more of a scream. I'm just as angry as he is, but bringing Philip into this is a low blow.

"I think you convinced yourself that the only way you deserved to live while he was gone was if it was some fairytale. But we were never going to own a mansion. Not from where we started. And even if we did, I'm sure you would've set your eyes on another mountain to drag us up." I try to speak over him to explain just how wrong he is, but he yells over me. "And honestly, I think the only thing worse than that radio message being a lie would be making it to the equator and watching you realize you're still just as fucking miserable."

The thought that I'm just some drill sergeant, forcing Sebastian to endure my endless conquests takes the energy out of me. Because that's what he thinks of me. At his core. Just some broken, miserable boy. "Fine. Say you're right. I'm a monster carrying you along. Have you ever stopped to wonder why you are dragging your feet in the face of oblivion? Ever wondered why, if I'm so awful, you stuck around without saying a word?"

The heat leaves his face, and I'm sickened that his pained expression makes me happy. "I was just trying to make sure we enjoyed ourselves a little bit. Help some people along the way. Just in case there aren't any planes. Just in case this is the end. Because if this is it, when the White gets us, you aren't going to be thinking about how close you got to saving us. You are going to be thinking about how all we did was run away."

"If we're just going to die in the end, it doesn't matter. Don't you get that?"

"White or no White, one day, we are going to die. Just like Philip and all the people who met the White before us. This is all we have. So why not help some poor assholes out? Why not, instead of rushing from one place to another, we enjoy ourselves?"

I sit on the ground. I feel like I'm going to be sick. He can't be right. No. I wasn't trying to make us miserable. I was trying to save us. "Every bad experience we had. Everything we survived. It can't just be a grain of sand in this cruel world. It has to mean something. It's awful enough when we get a full boring life. At least then, we have a choice. This. This though. This is meaningless. It doesn't matter. It's just sad and awful and unfair. So yes, I believe the impossible because it's the only thing keeping me going."

He sits next to me. "It does matter. It does. To us. That's the only people who it ever mattered to. Yeah. We can kick and scream or sit down and enjoy the breeze. Neither are going to stop this. But it means we get to spend a day enjoying the breeze. So, I'm going to try to help those people. I'm going to do what I have to do to live with myself. But I won't blame you for doing what you have to do."

"If you think I'm awful enough to desert you—if you think so low of me—what's kept you here all this time as I drag you along. Huh?" I don't know what I think or feel. I just need to know why.

He stares up to the sky to try to stop the tears from spilling over. "Because I love you." He gets up. Kisses my head. "I don't think you're a monster. I think you're hurt. Been hurt for a long time. But I won't leave those people to die. Maybe I will get killed in the process. But I have to do it. Same reason you have to reach Miami. But if there isn't anything there, I want you to get in the water. Enjoy yourself before the White gets to you. Okay?"

He reaches for me, but I recoil. He unstraps the rifle, sets it on the bike, and walks away toward the exit.

Everything he's said swirls in my mind. It's all so different from what I experienced that I don't know how to consolidate his recollection with my own, and maybe it's because a part of me knows, even if he misinterpreted half of it, that he's at least a little right. Maybe losing Philip, knowing how fragile this life was, put a fire in me to make something great out of my life. Maybe that fire burned too bright for me to see everything we had. But I was never too good for Sebastian. I couldn't leave him here. Because he was the only constant. From holding me on his bedroom floor to fighting me every step of the way on the road.

A plane to Miami doesn't matter if he isn't on it.

I stand, but he isn't in eyesight. I sat there longer than I thought. I dart toward the exit on foot, screaming for him. "Sebastian!"

As I start down the exit, I see him. He's past the exit ramp, walking down the street. He turns back toward me. He's crying.

"Sebastian, I—"

But then, he's gone, obscured by a white truck that pulls out from a side street and blocks the road between us. The bearded man, and he isn't alone. The pious woman from the warehouse steps out of the vehicle with a gun trained on Sebastian. I dash for the rifle. By the time I turn back toward them, they have him in the cabin, and they're speeding off.

They have him.

I try to scream—to curse the White and these lunatics and myself for not acting faster—but the air refuses to enter my lungs. I can't breathe. I waver, fall backward, and hit the blacktop. The world spins.

No. Not now.

I force myself to sit up. Drop the rifle. Jam my shaking hand into my pocket. I grab the pin and begin stabbing. Over and over. But it doesn't work. My legs and arms are already numb from the oxygen deprivation. It's useless. Maybe it always was. I toss it into the road, and I regret doing so the second it's gone.

Everything is going black when Sebastian's words return to me. "Breathe with me. In. Out."

I close my eyes.

We're back on his bedroom floor.

His palm is on my chest, and we still think we are going to conquer the world.

"In. Out."

I follow his words.

In.

Out.

I keep doing it until my lungs replenish and the feeling in my extremities returns.

I silently thank him and open my eyes.

The White fills the sky overhead. It'll be here soon, and those lunatics have Sebastian. My best friend, my lover, my ex, and the only person I want beside me in the end.

I get to my feet. Collect the rifle. Get back on the bike and start the engine. I drive back into Charlotte in the direction the truck went. I'm going to save him or die trying. I love him, and I'd rather argue with him the whole way to Ecuador than spend a single second of what's left of my miserable life without him.

PART SEVEN

LINGER

I

Right or left.

Last I saw the truck, it cut down this side street, but from the fork it splits into, I have no clue which way it went. They could've taken him to the parking garage or that warehouse or another location we didn't discover.

Every second I linger, Sebastian is one step closer to being sent into the White. Its power is more tangible this close. Leaves tear off the few plants that aren't bare, and trees and street signs waver under its force. But its gravitational force pales in comparison to the kaleidoscope of every trial and tribulation I've ever experienced that it presents to me.

Sebastian—in that truck, in a cattle car—keeps me grounded. The clock is ticking down until the White nears the border of the city. It's time to act.

I take the path right, aiming for the warehouse, the closer of the two locations where I know they're holding people. On the bike, with the roads clear, I make it there in a matter of minutes.

Even with the rushing wind overtaking the silence of the city, as if the buildings themselves are whining under the pull of the White, I stop the bike a block before the warehouse so that I don't risk them hearing the engine. I make it over to the shrubs we crouched behind before. Through the shaking branches, I spot a cattle car attached to a truck near the road, but the truck is red, not white. A bulbous man is waving on a semi-truck that is being backed out of another garage door. I don't want to think about how many people it could contain.

Sick fucks.

At this rate, they'll be shipping their sacrifices out in no time. But the white truck isn't in sight. Sebastian must be somewhere else. I breathe through the mounting panic that I won't get to him. I'll be useless to him dry heaving in a ball on the ground. *In. Out.* I continue the deep breaths as I jog back to the bike and set out for the parking garage.

II

I reach the parking garage in no time. The drivers seem too busy finishing preparations to patrol. Just off the street before the garage, I kill the engine. I wheel the bike across the street from the entrance and park it behind one of the cars pushed up on the sidewalk.

The ground floor of the parking garage is empty, but the distant sound of a running engine echoing from the building is audible. I can't make out anything on the second floor, and without Sebastian's binoculars, I don't have a great chance of seeing much. The only way I'm going to know if I'm hearing the bearded man's truck is by reentering the garage.

I'm making sure the rifle is loaded when a memory worms its way into my mind. The first Thanksgiving after we moved closer to Trinity. Our families switched off every year between my house and Sebastian's since neither of our mothers would agree to fully relinquish the reins of the holiday to the other. This one was at Sebastian's parent's house. I held his hand under the table as he told them we were more than just friends.

My mother's congenial demeanor cracked. Sebastian's father smacked the table, screaming that this better be the worst joke Sebastian ever told. The ensuing chaos that became the last time either of us spoke with our parents plays back in my mind in HD. No calls attempted on either end, even after the White arrived. We were already dead to them.

Below it all, it's almost like I can hear the White whispering to me. Offering to consume these horrible morsels. Wrap me in its tendrils and cradle me until I fall asleep and am freed from this painful little life.

I keep thinking of Sebastian. Not that awful dinner. Where he might be now. And my promise at the farmhouse to keep him safe. If he's on the second floor of this parking garage, we're only minutes from reconnecting. A tether, holding me down to the present and keeping me from floating off into the White.

I make sure I have plenty of bullets before I cross the street and head into the garage. After a quick sweep of the first level, which looks as empty as before, I make a beeline for the second floor. I hug the wall on the bend so that should a truck or van come rushing down, I won't be an easy target. The engine grows louder as I near the level. Over the top of the incline, a light-colored truck is near the cattle car. I hurry the rest of the way to the level and duck behind the closest pillar to my left.

I peek around the cement square. A beige truck that has wheels far larger than the one the bearded man drove is parked. The cattle car isn't hooked up to it, and no one is in the cabin. A man kneels by the tire that Sebastian slashed. Tools and a spare are spread out around him. Another thinner man stands behind him with a sawed-off shotgun.

Sebastian isn't here. I bite back the urge to scream. But the truck isn't running, and still, the engine hums and exhaust spills out from the side of the cattle car. Another vehicle is behind it. The vehicle turns, and the men are bathed in red light before the yellow beams of headlights shine in the opposite direction. The vehicle pulls out from around the cattle car. I'm hoping with such fervor it's a white truck that I can practically see it, which only makes the sight of the maroon van more crushing.

The lights rush toward my location. I pull back against the pillar and crack my head against the stone in my rush. The shock of the pain, coupled with the knowledge that if Sebastian isn't being held here, then I have no clue where to find him, makes me lose my nerve. Tears well up in my eyes. I fight back a sob. *In. Out.* This can't be how we go. I have to find him. I just have to.

The van nears the pillar, and I should walk around the outside to avoid being seen in passing, but the thought enters my mind when it's already driving past. A gray-haired woman I haven't previously seen is in the driver's seat, and the old man from the cattle car sits beside her in the passenger's seat. I have little doubt as to how he bargained for his freedom. The drivers knew right where to find us.

Still, after all they went through to get back that woman and her child, I can't imagine these psychos are eager to distribute Get Out of Jail Free cards. Maybe a trade? Two sinners for the price of one born-again follower.

I could aim a bullet at the passenger's seat through the back window. Kill that fucking traitor. The image of the glass fracturing around the bullet meant to end his life is so vivid that it almost seems like a path that is already laid out for me. All I have to do is follow suit. Pull the trigger and watch the white smoke emit from the end of the rifle. Play my God-damn part and—

I stop myself. Come back from whatever the hell that urge was to act recklessly. The likelihood of it hitting him is slim. Plus, getting even isn't going to help me find Sebastian. I'll probably just end up finding the wrong end of that shotgun.

I have to think. Driving through the city, avoiding these drivers, and happening upon the truck is also unlikely. I wish I could climb into the back seat of that maroon van, press the rifle against the woman's skull, and demand to know the other locations. Cornering one of them is probably my only way of finding out, and I don't love the idea of trying to pick off one of the men near the cattle car before they shoot me or alert the others on the radio.

That's it.

I hightail it back to the first level. The van driver has to stop at some point to let out the old man. Or she's taking him to another location. Either way, tailing them seems like a better option than taking my chances with the other two men. The van is only pulling onto the street when I make it around the bend to the first level. I haven't lost them yet.

I dash for the entrance. Once they are farther down the road, I cross the street and get the bike. I don't waste a second trying to catch my breath. I start the engine. I'm flying down the road when they turn right onto a side street. I keep one turn behind them. All the way to a residential street a few blocks away.

The van stops in front of a row of townhouses. This far from the main streets and exits, the road is littered with parked cars that are still on the road. I hide the bike between a hatchback and a two-door in front of a neat, identical row of townhouses. I take the rifle in my hands and remove the safety. Around the side of the hatchback, I catch the old man hobbling up the sidewalk to a brick house with green shutters that is sandwiched between two with beige siding. The woman stays in the vehicle.

The man bends over a wilted flower bed near the door, clutching the small of his back as he searches among the surrounding rocks in the landscaping with the other. He straightens with a rock in hand. I expect him to break a window until he turns it over and pulls a key from a compartment in its bottom. He retreats through the front door.

They're making a stop. I'm surprised the woman would trust him in there alone, but it's not like he can run for it. There aren't enough parked cars leading up to the van for me to sneak up on her. Furthermore, she'd have easy access to her radio to sound the alarm in the vehicle. But if the man doesn't come out of the townhouse, she'll have to go inside to collect him . . .

The rest of the plan writes itself, and I have no more time to waste on doubt. I run around the side of the nearest townhouses to the backyards. Each row has its own fence, sectioning off the yards in squares. Past it is a thin patch of woods that doesn't quite block out a main road, at least not at this time of year. The first group of townhouses are encased in wrought-iron fences with pointed spikes. While the shut front doors look undisturbed, the sliding glass doors in the back are all shattered. The drivers probably went through these places.

The house the old man went inside farther down the street has a tall, wooden fence. My breaths come out in white puffs as I run. When I slow near it, I see the fence is made of plastic, not wood. The open gate leads me to a yard of overgrown, yellow grass. There's a jungle gym in the center and a charcoal grill up the stairs, on the back porch.

The sliding door is hollow, and the glass it once contained is sprinkled all over the porch and what looks like the kitchen floor inside. I take a second to catch my breath so that my heaving doesn't give me away. The glass bits, illuminated in the White light, sparkle like diamonds in a jewelry commercial. Little jewels presented on velvet backdrops. I try to think of the names of those stores. Not how when I walked out to the highway two nights after Philip was run over, there was still debris remaining on the side of the road. *Zales. Jared. King's. Kay.* Not how, at that late hour, there was no traffic, and when I held a shard of glass in my hand, it cut my palm, and the pain rippled through my body like a jolt of lightning that I enjoyed every time I used it to cut myself in the early years.

No.

The White's going to have to try harder than that if it's going to stop me from getting to Sebastian. *In. Out.* I pick the spots on the kitchen floor that have the least amount of glass. I carefully step inside to keep the sound of crushing glass low. There's a doorway ahead of me as well as one to my right. I go through the entrance in front of me. I should start at the closest point to the front door and work my way back from there to ensure he doesn't get back to the woman before I find him.

The White seeps through the sheer gingham curtains ahead of me and lights a dining room. The van outside is a red blob through the fabric that looks more like a blood stain than a vehicle. A long wood table sits at the center of the room with matching chairs. A china cabinet is against the wall, containing decorative plates. No old man. I cross to the other side of the room and head into the entryway. The front door is shut. I don't see him anywhere. A creak comes from directly above me. He's upstairs.

I can't seem to get control of my breathing. I slowly funnel the air through my nostrils to make it as quiet as possible. On the other side of whatever happens in this house, Sebastian is waiting for me.

I pass a TV room to my left on my way down the hall to a stairwell. The dark wood stairs jut straight up to the second floor with a sharp turn left toward the top. There must be no windows near it above because darkness envelopes the turn. I hold my breath to listen for the old man, but I can't hear anything. I check the rifle to make sure the safety is off in case I somehow noted it incorrectly the first time. It's off.

I mind the picture frames lining the wall as I go up the stairs. I make a quick turn and continue up the last few steps. A short hallway. Light radiates from under the doorways, but it is still darker than I've grown accustomed to this close to the White. Most of the light is coming from the open door at the end of the hall. I can only make out more stairs that lead up to a third floor. An attic.

I cross the hallway and stop at the door. I can hear the old man talking above. "Come on, Elaine." I freeze. The woman in the van. Did she follow him in after I ran for the back door? I don't think I saw a silhouette through the curtains on the first floor. All I remember is the deep red stain.

Two versus one isn't great odds.

In.

Out.

The old man wasn't armed. And I still have the element of surprise on my side. And as long as the woman doesn't shoot me, I can overpower them. I have to keep moving. I take the first step and it creaks so loud that it must be what I heard on the first floor. The old man falls silent.

Shit.

I consider retreating and regrouping, but there isn't time. Whatever is up there, I must face it. I take the stairs two at a time, and I don't tread lightly. They know I'm here. The wood creaks beneath my step. The ledge to my left lowers to the wood floor of the attic as I climb. A bedroom lit with tall windows around the room. A bed against one wall and a dresser and nightstand on the other. The old man stands beside a trunk alone in the corner, staring out a window. No woman in sight. She must still be in the van. Something about his averted stance is more unnerving than having him face me.

I aim the rifle at the middle of his back. "Turn around!"

He doesn't move.

Considering the direction of the staircases, the window he's standing at faces the road out front. He could be trying to alert the woman. "Back away from the window now, or I'll shoot."

The old man turns around. He doesn't appear shocked to see me, and the pointed gun doesn't faze him. He looks more sad than anything. "You have to understand that I—"

"I don't have to understand shit," I tell him. The idea that he is going to make me understand anything after betraying us, when Sebastian still had every intention of saving him, just proves how little we can trust anyone. Had those drivers not known where to find us, who knows where we'd be now. "You are going to sit down and wait for your friend to come inside. Or I can shoot you dead, and I can get her in here faster."

He sucks his teeth, mulling over my words. "She's no friend of mine. I'll do whatever you want. Just help me pull this aside."

He points to the trunk beside the wall.

I can't think of anything I would rather do less. "Is that where you're hiding your plane?"

"How'd you know?" He matches my sarcasm. "Now push . . . or pull."

"You must've fucking lost it in that cattle car if you think I'm doing anything for you, you piece of shit!" I'm screaming. I take a breath.

"This used to be my home. I—"

"Sit down and shut up."

"My granddaughter, Elaine, loved it here because there was a storage cubby behind this chest. A little door perfect for an eight-year-old. When they took me and my daughter, we hid her up here with all the food and water we had. I have to—"

"So, selling us out wasn't enough? You want to kill her, too?" I want to push him out one of the windows.

Now, he looks angry, his wrinkled skin drawing toward the bridge of his nose in a scowl. "Her father was out foraging. He probably came for her. But if not, she isn't going to know the White is here. If she's still locked in, I have to get her out and warn her. I'm telling that whacko out there that she's gone either way. I'd never give her up to them."

"But you're fine selling out strangers who were going to help you," I reply.

"You and I both know you had no intention of returning for us." The old man checks the window and begins pulling at the one end of the chest to try to slide it out from the wall.

I watch him carefully. One wrong move, and I'll shoot. "Maybe I wouldn't. But Sebastian, he would. He was foolish enough to think you were good. Now, they have him."

The chest doesn't move an inch. He stands, winded. "What do you want, an apology? In my shoes, you would've done the same thing. Now help me with this God-damn chest or all of it was for nothing."

"So you can try to take the rifle while I do?" I move the barrel to his head, and his unflinching reaction angers me. "Or I can shoot you. Because you betrayed us, and after that woman comes in, I'm going to get the other locations of where they're holding people, and I'm going to shoot her, too. Then, I'm going to leave here and never think about it again, because you both are pieces of shit."

He rubs his chin, unbothered. "It'll alert the cuckoo clock outside, who'll call for backup. And you haven't killed a man. If you had, then I'd already be dead. I probably deserve it. Most people left do."

"Not Sebastian," I say, and even speaking his name makes me want to scream. Makes me want to be the person who could just shoot this old man and walk away.

"Not Elaine either. You help me move this, and I'll help you find him."

"Why the fuck do you think I can trust you?"

"You can't, but once I make sure Elaine is safe, I don't care what happens to me. I did you wrong, and believe it or not, that matters to a man like me. If I can screw over some of these idiots on the way out, then I'd be happy to do so. Now help me move this thing. Weighs a ton." He pulls on the chest again, his back to me.

I know Sebastian would trust the old man if he were here. I also know I can't. Still, the old man knows this city like the back of his skeletal hand, and that'll be useful when I get the addresses of the other holding locations from the woman.

"You pull anything, you're dead."

He's still struggling with the chest. "Great. Now help."

I keep the rifle in my hands. I go to the other side of the chest and press my boot into the side to push it. It doesn't move. I take one hand off the rifle and push. It slides ever so slightly. He's not lying—it's heavy. I push harder, and with the old man pulling, it slides aside to uncover a door at knee height.

"Elaine, it's Papa," says the old man, in a softer tone than I thought his scratchy voice could produce.

The door is painted the same cream color as the walls, and other than a small, golden knob and a thin dark seam around the square, it could be easily overlooked, especially with a chest in front of it. I wonder how long the old man was in that cattle car. I wonder how much food they gave the girl. I wonder if the girl's father was also captured, if the girl didn't have the strength to push past the chest, and what horrors await us inside the storage space.

I take a step back.

The old man bends over and yanks the door open. "Elaine?"

Rot wafts from the space. I can only see the ends of some cartoon fleece blanket on the ground. The old man repeats himself. His top half disappears inside the door. "Elaine, are you there?"

The space looks too dark to see clearly, and the woman in the van could be here any minute. I grab my flashlight. "Here. Use this."

The man turns to me, and I watch the tidal wave of fear of what he may find crash over his face. He must smell it too. He takes the flashlight, and he pauses for a moment before turning it on. I should look away, but I don't want to put my back to him. A *The Little Mermaid* blanket is bunched up on the floor. Food containers and plastic wrappers are littered around it. The old man holds one hand on the wall for support as he bends over and looks left into the space where apparently the storage room continues. A sudden inhale.

He staggers back into the chest. I steady him. Tears wet his face when he hands me back the flashlight. But he's smiling.

He must've cracked.

"Are you okay?"

"Nothing in there but old food and piss and shit," he says. "Always said that girl had atomic diapers."

I don't mention that many people other than the girl's father could've taken her. He must see the doubt on my face because he explains, "She was obsessed with her Raggedy Andy doll. Wouldn't let it leave her side day or night. My daughter could barely get it off her to wash it when it was stained. Had they taken her, they wouldn't have let her take it. They barely let me keep the clothes on my back when they locked me up. Her father must've got her. She's safe."

I don't know why the idea of her dying in there seems far more believable than her being safe and sound. Regardless, I have enough sense to keep it to myself. "I'm glad. I—"

Beep!

The sound startles us both. The woman outside. She's getting impatient.

"Time to hold up your end of the bargain," I tell him.

His hopeful face deflates.

"You aren't seriously backing out," I start.

He waves a hand to silence me. "You know you'll have to kill her? Or she'll get word back to them before we reach another location."

I glance out the window, but all I can see is the top of the red van. She'd probably do worse if the roles were reversed. "I know."

He joins me at the window. "And you're prepared to do that?"

You fucking shot me!

The man's words from the gas station return to me. The anger. The pain. Caused by my hand. I killed him. Maybe not directly, but I saw him all the same in my dreams each night. Shooting her outright. Killing her. That'll haunt me for the rest of my life. But there's no other option. Tying her up and hoping she doesn't get out of the storage space is too risky. I can't squander my last chance to save Sebastian. "I'll do whatever it takes to get him back."

We discuss what happens next. We just need to lure her inside and far away from the car radio. After we restage the attic, we head downstairs. He follows, and I know he could turn on me at any stage of this plan. I rub the back of my head to block a blow. Should he betray me, I need to be ready to act. I turn to make sure we haven't missed anything on the way down the steps and to keep an eye on him. My gaze goes to the silhouette of porcupine yarn hair belonging to a doll beneath the bed. Raggedy Andy. I keep the observation to myself, and whether it's for his sake or that of our plan, I'm not sure.

III

I hear the old man's voice first. Somewhere on the first floor, too far out of range for me to make out his words. I stand in a bathroom. Hexagonal mustard tiles cover the walls and floor. A counter with a shallow sink rests against the wall with narrow wooden drawers below it. Against the far wall, there's a clawfoot tub. Little orange triangles in the white coating cry streaks of rust down the sides of the tub. The frosted glass window above it looks more like a strangely placed LED light fixture with the White shining through it.

The stairs groan as they make their way up. The old man could've sold me out, but then he and the woman would've probably just left me here. He also has something to gain. Without me, he'll ride with the woman back to the cattle car.

I concentrate on their voices instead of how I could probably find facial-hair scissors, fingernail clippers, cuticle trimmers, tweezers, or something else in this bathroom sharp enough to cut open my thigh and use the pain to quell my nerves. They could hear me. I don't need it. I just need to breathe.

In.

Out.

"Feel truly grateful that your reunion in heaven shall be immediate," says the woman. "Absolved from mortal sin in your sacrifice and granted entry into the land of the faithful." The genuine kindness and softness in her voice makes me nauseous. I wonder how many people this demented

Pied Piper led to their death with that voice. No matter how awful what I'm about to do is, she's the true monster.

"I'm just glad to have her back with me," the old man says, so clear that they must be outside the door.

I hold my breath again. The stairs creak as they ascend to the attic. The woman's words drift out of earshot. Now is the time to act. To open the bathroom door and do what needs to be done to get Sebastian back. I know that. I know he's gone if I don't, but I stay there for a moment. Maybe it's because I want to live another few seconds in this half of my life. The half before I cross that line and become the person who can kill someone else. Who will probably have to kill more people before I reach Sebastian. I don't try any more deep breathing. There is no making this better. There is just getting through it.

The footsteps above are distant. They must be at the chest. I can't wait any longer. I open the door slowly without a sound. I step into the hall, go to the doorway of the attic, and climb the stairs.

What happens within feels like it lasts centuries, each second spanning lifetimes. But once it's done—the rifle fired, the woman gargling for air from the shot that was meant for her head but hit her throat—it all comes back in distant actions. Stage directions in a scene from some old play your high school English teacher makes you perform in the front of the class.

As soon as I make it up the stairs, I have the gun aimed at her before she can pull the handgun from her hip holster. The old man takes it from her. Words are exchanged. Insults of how the White will cleanse us filth and how she will be rewarded, even if I strike her down.

The old man shoots her in the hand, scalping her thumb and leaving her pointer finger hanging on to the rest of her by a sliver of tendons and flesh. I push down the rising vomit. I go with it like it's part of our plan. I promise a slow, painful death unless she talks. She remains tightlipped, even after I shoot her in the calf. Blood leaks from the hole in her tattered leather boot.

Pleas for mercy. Prayers to Jesus, Mary, and God. I step on her wounded hand and aim the rifle at her other palm that she raises above her in defense. I tell her I'll shoot her again and again. I tell her that if she passes out, we will wrap her wounds and wake her up and continue. Because I'm not going to stop until she talks.

Tears soak her face. A final prayer of forgiveness before she rattles off the list of addresses between shallow breaths. I look at the old man to confirm he has them because I can't think of anything except ending this. I aim for her head, but I close my eyes when I pull the trigger. It misses its mark. I'm reloading when she chokes on the blood pouring from the wound and falls still.

IV

The next thing I know, we are back on the ground floor. I look out the window in the dining room. All I can see above the nearby buildings is the White. It's so bright that, even squinting, I can barely see the clouds within moving. I'm shaking. The rifle is in my hands, and the handgun is looped in my belt. A hand touches my shoulder. I turn to find the old man, hovering in the darkness of my unadjusted vision.

"You alright?" he asks.

I return my focus to the White. "What do you think it is?"

"I don't know," he says thoughtfully. "It could've been waiting below the surface ever since we were apes, and something triggered it. Or it's from some other place. I doubt knowing one way or the other is going to stop it. We better get a move on. It's getting close."

He's right.

I clear my throat. I explain that I've already crossed out the warehouse and parking garage. "What else do we have left?"

He repeats the addresses slowly, seemingly connecting them to his mental map of the city. "Another parking garage and a freight transport company building."

"Freight transport?"

"Semi-trucks, etcetera."

A building full of semi-trucks. "How many people could they keep in a place like that?"

"More than I'd like to think about, but I doubt they'd keep too many there." He turns his milky eyes away from the light coming in the window.

"If they have enough semi-trucks, why not just keep everyone there?"

"Well, twenty malnourished escapees are easier to manage than two hundred. Maybe they were worried if they put too many of us in one place, the prisoners might start looking more like an army."

I can't argue with that. I push through the fog that's overtaken my mind since the attic. We need every second we can get to reach Sebastian. "Which one is closer?"

"Two separate directions. Both around ten or so minutes away from here."

"North and south?" We could go for the one closest to the White.

"East and west."

Another crossroad. Right or left. The minutes are melting away. They'll be sending them out into the White before very long if their harebrained idea is to stop it from consuming the city. I need to choose. I wish for some gut feeling or sign from the universe to tip the scale one way or the other. Nothing comes to me. Just a decision I may regret for the rest of my miserable life. A coin toss. I say the first that comes to mind. "Freight transport. If there is no white truck, we are going to the garage. Come on."

The old man trails behind me to the bike, holding on to anything he can find along the way to steady himself. He's weak. Who knows the last time he ate. After I turn the key in the ignition, I reach into a side bag, pull the first thing I find—a bag of pretzels—and hand it back to him. Over the rushing wind, I scream, "Here, but I need the directions fast as we go."

The old man rips open the bag and pulverizes a pretzel in my ear in a matter of seconds. "Head back up this street."

V

The old man barks directions into my ear as I go. I drive as quickly as I can while still maintaining balance as the White pulls us toward it. An ancient whale opening its mouth to inhale a school of guppies that are trying to swim against the rushing water.

Right.

Another block down.

Left.

I try to concentrate on the old man's words through the tug of war of past mistakes and future calamities that overwhelm my mind. Every misstep and regret funneling to Sebastian's demise. Had I waited a little longer to tell him I planned on leaving. Had I not lost my temper in that last argument. *Left here.* Had I realized how stupid I was acting before he had a chance to walk down the exit and into the arms of these lunatics. Choosing this freight transport instead of the garage. *Two more blocks.* Never finding the cattle car or truck that he's on. Him disappearing into the White while I'm scurrying around in this rat maze.

The option of losing him—of our last exchange being all he has in the end—brings tears to my eyes. I blink through them. *Turn right up here.* I repeat the directions in my mind. I have to get to the freight transport building. Losing him isn't the end of our story. He isn't going to disappear on me. I'm going to save him. There's still time.

In.

Out.

I steady my breath and ask, "How close are we?"

"It'll be just up here on the left, another light before the exit," the old man says.

A short route to the highway and then into the White. I see why they picked the spot. Thankfully, no semi-trucks pull onto the road ahead of us. A square brick building comes into view down the road. It's flanked on either side by gates that lead into a gravel parking lot behind the building that is encased in what looks like a twelve-foot tall, chain-link fence.

There's a single green car out front, but nothing else I can make out.

"My buddy, Michael Randolph, trucked for a little over a decade." He stifles a burp. "Four loading docks in the back and probably a few trucks."

Plenty of room for the bearded man and the pious woman to bring Sebastian right to the truck. I pull into the parking lot of a bank that looks like it was vacant long before the White was discovered. Faded paint and splintered plywood over the windows. I park on the opposite side of the structure, under a covered drive-through that was probably for quick withdrawal and deposits when it was open.

"Stay put," I tell the old man. I pull the keys out of the ignition and start around the side of the building. I want to get eyes on that back lot. I don't have much time left to reach the other parking garage if I made the wrong choice.

Through the parking lot, there's a hill spotted with leafless greenery. It hides the freight transport building and the lot behind it. I jog up the red dirt to the top. Bare branches cling to my clothes as I climb. I push past them until I can see over the top. A parking lot expands behind the freight transport building. Dark streetlights pepper the large space. There's a blue truck and black car toward the back of the lot, and right next to one of the open garage doors, a white truck is parked with the rear fender smashed in. There is no mistaking it for another. It belongs to the bearded man.

Sebastian's here. The relief is immediate, but he is far from safe. I've barely turned back around to go down and tell the old man the good news when I hear an engine. I hurry farther over the mound to get a better look at the back of the building. Exhaust spits from the open garage door at the end. Then, two massive red eyes glow from within. Taillights.

They're leaving.

They're driving a semi-truck into the White.

And Sebastian is trapped inside.

I found him, and just like that, he's slipping through my fingers like water.

My initial instinct is to run toward it. Shoot the drivers, grab Sebastian, and go. An urge so overpowering that, like the impulse to shoot at the red van in the parking garage, I can already see myself running down the hill. But I know that's a stupid idea. I know I'll never get down the hill and over the fence on foot.

I can't tell if this means I'm truly losing it, or if the White is trying a new tactic to get to me. Either way, now isn't the time to dwell on it. I need the bike if I'm going to stop this truck. Everything else is a lower priority.

I take off back down the hill and around the building to the bike. The old man has a water bottle in his one hand as he straddles the bike. He raises his hands, saying, "I was choking and I—"

"He's here!" I call, shooing him to get off the bike. "He's here and they're leaving. Get off. I need to go. Now."

The man swings his leg off the bike and almost falls, catching himself on the wall of the building. "What's the plan?"

"I'm going to stop them." I turn the key, and the engine roars to life.

"How?" the old man asks.

"I don't know. I can't let them get away." The kickstand is up, but the old man is in front of the bike. "Step aside. I have to go."

"It'll blow right through you if you try to block its path."

The moment before Philip's impact consumes my mind. Not that I witnessed it. One created in sleepless nights when I wondered if he'd known what was going to happen. I decided that he had—a second too late. His face turned toward the truck right before his life was torn to pieces. A brief, terrible realization that he was going to die and that he couldn't do anything about it.

The strange reality that I'm returning to that instant, only a few minutes before I meet the semi-truck, with a desire to be between it and its destination, isn't lost on me. But I'm not going to just throw myself in front of it or try to block it. "I'll take out the wheels. Or the driver. It is none of your business either way. I won't get a chance to stop them before they make it out of the gates if you don't move."

He sets his jaw. "When I went back up to the attic, I saw the Raggedy Andy doll. If they have her, I have just as much to lose as you do."

The way he abruptly shot the woman makes far more sense now. But if he keeps this up, I'm going to miss my chance to reach the truck. I reverse out of the drive-through.

The old man gets back in front of the bike before I'm able to fully turn around. "How good of a shot are you with that rifle, son? Because you'll probably only get one or two shots if you're lucky. I grew up out in the country. Hunted with my father every morning before the sun came up to put food on the table for my family."

"I have to have a better shot than an old man with cataracts." I'm done talking. I rev the engine and tell him he has one more second to get out of my way before I mow him down. He's insane if he thinks I'm going to give away the rifle and put Sebastian's life in his hands, especially after he already betrayed us. "I can do it alone."

"I killed just as many deer before my parents realized I was nearsighted and got me glasses. All that changed was that the brown blur I shot was more defined. You have the handgun. Take it and buy me enough time at the gate to get into position. Who knows, you might be able to stop it alone, but two shots are better than one."

Right or left.

I've never wished more for the ability to stop time. Because I didn't trust that I had the shot. Because I'd shot some cans along the way, but I hadn't shot a moving target. Not one that was rushing toward me. Because I couldn't imagine putting Sebastian's life in anyone else's hands. Because I knew this was yet another crossroad I could remember fondly when I wrapped my arms around Sebastian at night or one that would drive me insane after I lost him. Because, of course, it was this man, who had his own motivations and who, not unlike me, put his best interests and those of his loved ones above everything else. Because I know what Sebastian would want me to do. Because the seconds are evaporating, and it's time to make a choice.

VI

As I peel out of the parking lot and onto the road, I pray I chose the right path. The gate on the far side of the building is already swinging open. The pull of the White is so strong that I feel like I'm flying toward it. I shoot past the building and stop the bike in the median lines on the road before the gate. Within, the semi-truck is waiting a few hundred feet away. I put up the kickstand and hop off the bike just in time for the gate to finish opening.

The semi-truck engine howls in front of me. The bearded man is at the helm, pale with a bloodied bandage wrapped around his arm. The pious woman sits beside him. He locks eyes with me first. His nostrils flare. The woman brightens when she sees me, excited by the prospect of taking out one more sinner before they drive into the White.

My body turns on me. Head swimming. Lungs starving. Heart pounding. It knows it could be mere moments from death, and it's turning on the host. I think back to Sebastian and me on his floor one last time to remind myself to breathe and to have a good memory in my mind in case this is the end.

Philip. Our parents. The White. The end of the world. Everything has led me to this moment, standing before the truck. I feel behind me for the gun I have lodged in my belt. When the moment comes, I won't have time for fumbling with it. "We need to talk!"

I don't know what I expect them to say. Part of me hopes the bearded man will put the truck in park, get out, and explain why the only way

I can atone for my sins is by joining Sebastian in the back of the truck. Make himself an easy target. But he doesn't move. The woman's lips part, and while I can't be sure from this distance what she says, the expelling of compressed air and rotation of the tires assure me it is something along the lines of "Drive."

Only, the truck isn't moving forward. It is receding into the lot. *Beep, beep, beeping* as it goes. I attempted to prepare myself for any outcome in this hastily made plan, but a retreat never crossed my mind. It doesn't make any sense.

I inspect my surroundings. The feeling of being exposed sets in. Of carelessly moving a chess piece forward on a board to only see your opponent smirk in response. But I don't find anyone in the windows of the building or in the surrounding area. I take a step back toward the bike. I make myself not reach for the gun. I resist—

The engine wails and rips my train of thought to pieces. The semi-truck barrels toward me and the bike. It seems impossibly slow at the start, but every second it is building momentum and devouring the distance between us. He was never retreating. He was just giving himself enough room to reach a speed that will demolish me.

I draw the handgun and aim my fire at the right wheel, hoping to send it crashing into the fence and stop it before it clears the gate. A spark as the first shot hits the fender. Another grazes the hubcap. The third into the bumper. Finally, the next hits the tire, and it explodes. The truck swerves right, but the bearded man straightens the wheel.

I aim the handgun at the window. I pull the trigger. *Click.* I'm out of bullets. I counted them after I handed the old man the rifle. Four shots. Even though I hit the tire, it won't stop them.

I'm going to die.

Maybe the old man didn't have enough time to get into position after all. Maybe he planned to aim for the wheel himself, and seeing it was useless, surrendered. The initial rage at his inaction bleeds away as I acknowledge that everything is ending. There's no sadness or anger left in me. Just a gnawing emptiness that every sacrifice—every late night, early morning, careful step, and calculated move—has been a waste. My life was always going to end in tragedy, and worse still, I lost Sebastian in the process.

I battle against the urge to shut my eyes. My body tenses in anticipation for impact. I look up at my executioners, and it's that very moment that the shot rings out.

Bang.

The top of the bearded man's skull separates from his head in an eruption of gore from which blood and brain matter shower the windshield. The wheel cuts left, and with the subsequent shot that hits the front left tire, the semi-truck swerves into the open metal gate. It barrels through it, takes out a flagpole in the yard, and only stops when it smashes into the front of the building. The bricks crumble around the front of the truck. Black smoke expands from the spot.

It takes me a moment to comprehend exactly what transpired. I'm alive. The old bastard still has a good shot. He saved my life. We stopped the truck.

I hear something behind me. The man slowly gets to his feet across the street, where he was hidden on the ground among a patch of overgrown grass. He's laughing.

We did it.

I turn back to the truck, almost expecting the back door to fling open and the prisoners to come running out. But they were just standing in a steel box that collided with a building. Those inside—Sebastian—could be hurt, and with the smoke billowing from the front of the truck, it could be seconds from catching fire.

The cabin doors remain shut. I run for the back of the truck. Shots ring out in front of me. A patch of dirt explodes to my right. Through the smoke, I see a figure leaning out of one of the windows. The old man returns fire, and I hop on the tailgate, grateful for the momentary cover. I grab the two black handles to open the doors, but they catch on the metal lock at the center with a circular keyhole. I know exactly who has the key.

"Cover me," I shout back to the old man.

He fires a shot over the truck. "Watch the windows."

I peek around the corner of the truck. The passenger's side door is now open, and the woman's leg hangs limp over the side of the seat. I look above me at the building, and I see that the shooter is a teenage boy. He has a semi-automatic rifle aimed right at me.

Bang.

He flies back like someone pulled him to the floor. I wouldn't even know he was shot if it wasn't for the pained screams that follow.

I don't see any other shooters. Crouching low to the ground, I go for the cabin of the truck. There's a pistol in the grass. The woman must've lost it in the crash. I grab it. The safety is already off. I lead with it as I round on the cabin.

The iron smell of blood hits me before I have a chance to inspect the carnage within. The bearded man leans over the steering wheel, blood dripping from his shattered skull. The pious woman is pinned to her seat by a shard of glass that disappears into her stomach. Her hands hover over it, unsure what to do.

"We were . . . saving . . . this city. You . . . faithless." She struggles to continue. She coughs and sprays the dashboard with blood.

Smoke wafts across the windshield from the front of the truck that disappears within the building. If whatever is causing it reaches the gas tank, then we are all goners. I have to hurry. The keys are still in the ignition. A round one dangles from the chain. I reach over her and take the keys with my free hand. I step back out. The woman reaches for me. All I feel is disgust. I slam the door on her.

The old man hollers something behind me. I follow his aimed barrel in time to see him put a shot through the chest of a woman in a denim dress who was carrying a shotgun and coming through the yard right toward me.

Without the door open, I'm visible to anyone left alive in the building. I run back around the truck, coughing on smoke. I steady my hands enough to put the key in the lock and turn it. I tuck the handgun into my belt. Then, I pull the handles and rip open the doors.

At least fifty people are crowded within. Several cover their eyes from the light. A few are holding on to others who were either injured in the crash or too weak to stay up otherwise. None of them run for the exit.

"We have to go. Now!" I call.

They start marching forward. The first one who reaches me is a middle-aged man who is as thin as a stick. I help him down. I search the crowd for Sebastian. But I don't locate him in the rush. A woman hands me a toddler, who I hold until she gets down. I move from face to face as I continue lending a hand. He has to be here. It wouldn't make sense for the bearded man to take him to another location.

However, as the crowd thins, I still can't find him. The other possibilities take shape in my mind, expanding in connecting threads like a cobweb. The bearded man and the pious woman deciding he was too much trouble to be sacrificed. Sebastian trying to grab the wheel or run and ending up on the wrong end of the pistol in my belt. The drivers having two trucks, one that already departed from this location. All leading to the same end—Sebastian's death.

Another thought comes to me then. It sounds like the voice in my head. But it's different. Too firm. The White. It asks me that if Sebastian is already gone, then what is left for me. It shows me the short path from my bike to the swirling clouds.

But self-destruction isn't a new concept to me. It's been there before the White ever neared. I know better than to listen to it. *In. Out.* I also know the old man and I just stole a meal from reaching the White, and it has to be displeased. Good. I hoped it fucking starves.

A woman slips on the tailgate and grabs my shoulder to steady herself, a little girl desperately clutching her hand. I hope it's the old man's granddaughter. I guide her the rest of the way down. More shots whiz by overhead. There must've been more of those drivers inside than we imagined. The old man returns fire. "Move!"

I gave him a box full of bullets, but he isn't going to be able to hold them off much longer. The prisoners scatter away from the building to find cover.

I search among the remaining occupants for him. Two men support a third with a bone sticking out of his calf. The one on the left is dressed in acid-washed jeans and an oversized shirt that look familiar. He lifts his head as they near the mouth of the cargo trailer. Long hair falls in front of a face that I could never forget. "Sebastian!"

He stares at me for a moment like he doesn't believe it. Like I'll disappear if he blinks. When I don't, a smile spreads across his face. "Help us get him down."

They place the man on the lip of the tailgate. He's ashen, soaked in sweat, and looks about a second away from passing out. His hair is gray and face lined, but otherwise, he shares the face of who must be his son beside Sebastian. There's no way we are going to be able to carry him far enough away from the shooting on foot.

"We can wheel him out of here on the bike." I pull the handgun out of my belt. Look at his son. "Can you cover me?"

"I don't know how to shoot."

Sebastian takes it from me. "Be careful."

I'm running, dodging around prisoners who are too weak to run away. The old man and two shooters in the building trade shots. A man in front of me gets caught in the crosshairs, and a bullet takes a chunk out of his shoulder. Before I reach for him, another woman is dragging him to his feet. I move faster and reach the bike.

There's no time to celebrate. I take the handles, put up the kickstand, and start wheeling it back through what's left of the crowd. The barrel of a rifle comes out of a cracked ground-floor window, pointing right at me. The glare of the White reflects off the glass, which makes what should be a glimpse into the building a mirror of the outside. I'm still considering whether I should hit the ground when shots ring out.

The window shatters. Sebastian is out from behind the semi-truck, emptying a clip into the direction of the shooter. I make it the rest of the way to the truck, heaving air. My surprise at Sebastian's aim must not be well hidden because he says, "Like I was getting out of my father's house without knowing how to shoot a handgun."

I pull him close. Kiss him. For a second, I think I made the wrong decision until he kisses me back. We pull apart. There's so much I want to say, but it'll have to wait. I steady the bike while Sebastian and the son guide the man into the seat. Now, we just need to make it out of here, and we'll be okay.

All I want to do is get Sebastian away from these lunatics and the gunfire. "If you want to drive him up the street, we'll follow behind you."

"No," Sebastian says. "We can do it together."

The gun is empty, but any of those fuckers we come across won't know it. I tuck it into my belt. Sebastian and I each take a handle while the son follows behind us. We barely make it ten feet from the truck when it explodes.

Everything happens so fast. The deafening sound. The heat. The force that throws us forward. I lose the handle of the bike and skid onto the blacktop, face first. My ears ring. Face burns. Blood gets in my one eye. I wipe it away. Turn on my back, searching for Sebastian. Smoke muddles the air and flames grow within the building. Him, the bike, the man, and his father are nowhere in sight.

I sit up. Pain surges through my chest. I try to breathe, but it makes the pain worse. Screams erupt from the building. Others are hacking. Everything sounds so distant. Like I'm underwater. There's a man beside me with a shard of metal through his eye socket. I get to my feet. "Sebastian!"

"Over here." I spot him almost across the street. The bike is on top of the father. Him and the man are lifting it off him. Holding my chest, I head over to him. Once the bike is off the father, I wheel it onto the grass. Sebastian and the son each lend the man a shoulder and help him over to me. A shot rings out next to us. The old man isn't too far away. I turn to see a woman fleeing the building, her clothes aglow with flames, fall to the ground.

"Are you okay?" Sebastian looks me over.

"Road rash. Maybe a broken rib or something. You?"

He raises his arm. It's skinned, but the wound isn't too deep. "I'm okay."

I wrap my arms around him, and before I know it, I'm sobbing into his shirt.

After the lunatics within the facility fled, were shot down, or burned, the surviving prisoners regrouped. Unfortunately, the old man's family wasn't among them. The fire continued eating away at the inside of the building. Sebastian and I handed out most of our resources to the starved crowd. A few prisoners went around to the parking lot in the back to try to get the vehicles so that they could work on stopping the other trucks and cattle cars. The old man, still determined to find his family, disappeared with them.

Sebastian and I sit across the street, each with a water bottle in hand, watching the last of the fire rage inside. The brick structure might be all that remains once it burns out.

"I plan on going with them when they get the vehicles," Sebastian says, his eyes not leaving the flames.

"I know." I take a gulp of water that helps the burning in my throat, but it doesn't get rid of the taste of ash. "I'm going, too."

He turns to me, eyes wide. "You don't have to go for my sake."

"I know," I repeat. "I want to. The thought of them driving you into it—I." I lose my grasp on the thought. Then, finally, I just say, "No one deserves that."

His free hand travels across the grass and finds mine. I take it. He asks, "Do you think we would've figured it out, ended up together, if the world wasn't ending?"

I lift his hand. Kiss it. For the first time in a long time, I don't lie to him. Or myself. "Probably not. I love you. Always will. But probably not."

"I didn't think so either," he admits with a loving squeeze of my hand. "So, what would we've done?"

"I would have gotten an office job. A big house. A cute guy who only likes me for my money. Maybe I would have a mid-life crisis after the inevitable divorce. Sell it all. Move to the middle of nowhere and do yoga." I laugh, and it hurts my chest. "God, that blast must've concussed me or something."

He's laughing, too. "Yoga?"

"In the middle of nowhere," I say. "What about you?"

"Work my way up at the restaurant. Host. Manager. Buy the place. Save up. Use the money to start a home decorating business. I could remodel your mansion once you move into the middle of nowhere to do your yoga."

"Would my place need renovating?" I ask in feigned offense.

"Complete overhaul. Tear it down to the foundation and rebuild it." He's laughing so hard that tears streak down his soot-covered face.

My eyes return to the flames in the building. He turns my head back to him and kisses me.

"Who knows. Maybe after our parents kicked the bucket, I, svelte from yoga, and you, dressed to the nines from decorating a mansion owned by one of the Real Housewives, meet up again at the funerals. A torrid love affair ensues." I can picture him. Sunglasses, some nice suit, as handsome as he was when we first embraced. More lines. Gray hair on the sides of his head that makes him look distinguished.

"Hot." He can't stop laughing.

Two vehicles drive through the gate.

The sight of them, and the thought of what we have yet to face, sobers us. I finish my water bottle and stuff it back in my bag to toss later. I used to be the person who cared where it ended up. Even if it doesn't matter now, I want to be him again. "After we stop those trucks, I'm going to go to Miami. Try to get on one of those planes."

"I know." He looks at me. "I think you are probably going to need backup."

I kiss him again. "Do you think this thing is going to stop at the equator?"

I expect an echo of my former response. A *probably not.* Instead, he kisses me again. "I hope so. I really do."

"I'm sorry about before. About everything," I say. "I was so wrong."

"Not that I'll ever admit it, but I might not have been as right about everything as I hoped either. Maybe I was too stuck in the present to consider where we were heading. Regardless, we fucked it up together. And aren't we lucky that the world is ending, and we're stuck together?"

"Yeah. We should start playing the lottery when that opens back up."

"Definitely." He stands and helps me to my feet.

I tell him I love him. He tells me he loves me. We get on the bike, and we follow behind the caravan toward the next location. When he pulls me close, I know it isn't for fear of falling off. It's because whether we die in Charlotte, Miami, or in our eighties in Ecuador, we love each other, and we are going to face whatever we find down the road together.

ACKNOWLEDGMENTS

I only thought the world was ending twice in my life: when my first, long-term relationship ended and when there was a global pandemic. Both of those events occurred around 2020, and subsequently, *What Remains* was born.

However, over the course of writing this book, the story grew and developed, as they often do, so I want to thank everyone who was there for the ride.

First, I want to thank my grandfather, Joe Lewis, who would definitely get a kick out of having the book dedicated to him and appearing in the acknowledgments.

Thank you for getting me hooked on reading books and watching TV shows and movies from an early age. You taught me there is always a place to escape to when times get tough. You handed me *The Stand* by Stephen King at an early age and discussed *The Walking Dead* with me each week. You also helped distract me from life's stresses on your porch, when you, Pall Mall in hand, recounted stories of how you outran the cops on your motorcycle in the backwoods of Butler, Pennsylvania, and theorized how we would survive the apocalypse. Your life and death color so much of this book. I love you.

I want to thank the friends and family who helped me write this book as well. Thank you, Timons Esaias, who provided feedback on an early drabble. Thank you, Caitlin Hensel, my writing partner, who kept me accountable with morning pages and helped me refine the plot. Thank you, Marisa Balatico, my pandemic roommate and friend, who has always supported my writing. Thank you, Patrick Beets, for the mechanical assistance. Thank you, Amber Beets, my mother, for providing feedback on the final draft. Thank you, Sean Lowers, my partner, for loving me and reading all my work before it sees the light of day.

I also want to thank Megan Matejcic, Sara Tantlinger, George Galuschak, and Jeffrey J. Niles—friends and family who have supported me over the years.

Finally, I want to thank everyone who enabled the release of this book. Thank you, Patrick Reuman, for first taking a chance on this story and making sure it found a great home. Thank you, Joe Mynhardt, Jaime Powell, and everyone at Crystal Lake Publishing for sharing *What Remains* with their readers.

ABOUT THE AUTHOR

Corey Niles was born and raised in the Rust Belt. A graduate of Seton Hill's MFA program, he has published over thirty works of short fiction and poetry, appearing in *Nightmare Magazine*, *Space and Time Magazine*, and *The Horror Zine*.

He is the author of *Blood & Dirt*, a novel, and *Death & Other Forms of Devotion*, a poetry collection. He lives in North Carolina with his partner, Sean, and a sizable army of cats and dogs.

THE END?

Not if you want to dive into more of Crystal Lake Publishing's Tales from the Darkest Depths!

Check out our amazing website and online store or download our latest catalog here.
https://geni.us/CLPCatalog

We always have great new projects and content on the website to dive into, as well as a newsletter, behind the scenes options, social media platforms, our own dark fiction shared-world series and our very own webstore. Our webstore even has categories specifically for KU books, non-fiction, anthologies, and of course more novels and novellas.

Readers...

Thank you for reading *What Remains*. We hope you enjoyed this novel. If you have a moment, please review *What Remains* at the store where you bought it.

Help other readers by telling them why you enjoyed this book. No need to write an in-depth discussion. Even a single sentence will be greatly appreciated. Reviews go a long way to helping a book sell, and is great for an author's career. It'll also help us to continue publishing quality books.

Thank you again for taking the time to journey with Crystal Lake Publishing.

You will find links to all our social media platforms on our Linktree page. https://linktr.ee/CrystalLakePublishing

Follow us on Amazon:

MISSION STATEMENT

Since its founding in August 2012, Crystal Lake has quickly become one of the world's leading publishers of Dark Fiction and Horror books. In 2023, Crystal Lake officially transitioned into an entertainment company, joining several other divisions, genres, and imprints, including Torrid Waters, Crystal Lake Comics, Crystal Lake Games, Crystal Lake Kids, and many more.

While we strive to present only the highest quality fiction and entertainment, we also endeavour to support authors along their writing journey. We offer our time and experience in non-fiction projects, as well as author mentoring and services, at competitive prices.

With several Bram Stoker Award wins and many other wins and nominations (including the HWA's Specialty Press Award), Crystal Lake Publishing puts integrity, honor, and respect at the forefront of our publishing operations.

We strive for each book and outreach program we spearhead to not only entertain and touch or comment on issues that affect our readers, but also to strengthen and support the Dark Fiction field and its authors.

Not only do we find and publish authors we believe are destined for greatness, but we strive to work with men and women who endeavour to be decent human beings who care more for others than themselves, while still being hard working, driven, and passionate artists and storytellers.

Crystal Lake Publishing is and will always be a beacon of what passion and dedication, combined with overwhelming teamwork and respect, can accomplish. We endeavour to know each and every one of our readers, while building personal relationships with our authors, reviewers, bloggers, podcasters, bookstores, and libraries.

We will be as trustworthy, forthright, and transparent as any business can be, while also keeping most of the headaches away from our authors, since it's our job to solve the problems so they can stay in a creative mind. Which of course also means paying our authors.

We do not just publish books, we present to you worlds within your world, doors within your mind, from talented authors who sacrifice so much for a moment of your time.

There are some amazing small presses out there, and through collaboration and open forums we will continue to support other presses in the goal of helping authors and showing the world what quality small presses are capable of accomplishing. No one wins when a small press goes down, so we will always be there to support hardworking, legitimate presses and their authors. We don't see Crystal Lake as the best press out there, but we will always strive to be the best, strive to be the most interactive and grateful, and even blessed press around. No matter what happens over time, we will also take our mission very seriously while appreciating where we are and enjoying the journey.

What do we offer our authors that they can't do for themselves through self-publishing?

We are big supporters of self-publishing (especially hybrid publishing), if done with care, patience, and planning. However, not every author has the time or inclination to do market research, advertise, and set up book launch strategies. Although a lot of authors are successful in doing it all, strong small presses will always be there for the authors who just want to do what they do best: write.

What we offer is experience, industry knowledge, contacts and trust built up over years. And due to our strong brand and trusting fanbase, every Crystal Lake Publishing book comes with weight of respect. In time our fans begin to trust our judgment and will try a new author purely based on our support of said author.

With each launch we strive to fine-tune our approach, learn from our mistakes, and increase our reach. We continue to assure our authors that we're here for them and that we'll carry the weight of the launch and dealing with third parties while they focus on their strengths—be it writing, interviews, blogs, signings, etc.

We also offer several mentoring packages to authors that include knowledge and skills they can use in both traditional and self-publishing endeavours.

We look forward to launching many new careers.

This is what we believe in. What we stand for. This will be our legacy.

Welcome to Crystal Lake Publishing—Where Stories Come Alive!